Equally proficient in Hindi and English, **Mridula Garg** has written in almost every genre—novels, plays, collections of essays and short stories, poems in Hindi and English, two memoirs of fellow writers and a travel account. Her novels—among them, *Chittacobra* (1979), *Anitya* (1980), *Kathgulab* (1996), *Main Aur Main* (1984) and *Miljul Mann* (2010)—have been translated into many languages, including Bengali, English, French, German, Japanese, Malayalam, Marathi, Odia, Punjabi, Russian, Tamil and Telugu.

Among the several awards and honours Mridula Garg has received are the Vyas Samman and the Sahitya Akademi Award. She also received the Hellman-Hammet Grant from Human Rights Watch, New York in 2001.

Chittacobra

MRIDULA GARG

Translated from the Hindi by the author

SPEAKING
TIGER

SPEAKING TIGER BOOKS LLP
125A, Ground Floor, Shahpur Jat, near Asiad Village,
New Delhi 110049

Originally published in Hindi in 1979
This translation published by Speaking Tiger Books in 2023

ISBN: 978-93-5447-410-1
eISBN: 978-93-5447-414-9

10 9 8 7 6 5 4 3 2 1

Typeset in Dante MT Std by SÜRYA, New Delhi

Printed at Shree Maitrey Printech Pvt. Ltd., Noida

To

My Fellow Wanderer

Prologue

If you would travel with me through time and space, you must hear me out.

Someone asks, 'Where does the road go?'

The answer: 'Nowhere. It stays where it is.'

Yes, it goes nowhere. Shall I call the road fortunate? Indifferent? Indolent? It does not move. It is silent, still, and stands arms akimbo. People stray into its embrace. It lets them. It does not care.

The travellers do not care either. They take refuge in the road's arms and trample its bosom, not even pausing to look at it properly; so intent are they on their journey. Can they be called fellow-travellers—travellers of the same road?

The road does not care. Why should it? It has no journey to make. It knows neither a beginning nor an end. It starts nowhere; it goes nowhere. It needs no fellow travellers.

I am like the road, indifferent to my end but not to the beginning. That I remember. Not one but many beginnings.

I can tell you when and how my journey began.

I want to.

I need a companion to travel with me but I have no destination in mind. I know that you cannot accompany me to the end, but stay for as long as the story lasts. I will try to finish it before the journey ends. Yours, I mean. My journey is one with the story. Once my tale is told, the journey will end. I will set aside a little time for you. After I finish telling my story, I will cross to the other side of the road and walk away. You will see me for a while before I vanish. No ill omen will blight your voyage, my fellow traveller. You will know nothing of my journey thereafter. I will walk alone, incognita. You shall be my fellow traveller, but not my fellow sufferer in hopeless waiting.

One more thing. I will try to relate the story from the beginning to the end, but I am confused. I cannot remember when he was and when he was not.

When did he first come into my life?

When exactly?

It is impossible for me to conceive of a time when he did not exist. How could I exist if he did not?

You will not mind, will you, if he is there throughout my story, from beginning to end?

1

'Look. There's a blue ring around the moon. A blue halo...why?'

'Happens.'

'When?'

'When a great soul is born.'

'You mean, a great soul is taking birth right at this moment? With us as witnesses! When the soul is born, will the halo disappear?'

'Yes.'

I burst out laughing.

'What's so funny?'

I kept on laughing. 'Will the great soul waft down from the moon?'

'No, from the womb. Surely one great soul is not such a tall order for a country where a child is born every ten seconds.'

'Then there should be a ring around the moon every night.'

'Do you look at the moon every night?'

'No.'

'So?'

'Yes…I have seen it for the first time tonight.'

'Aha, that means a great soul will be born as your child.'

'My child?'

'Yes, yours and mine.'

'How do you know?'

'Because. When two people love each other, the way we do, a great soul is born to them.'

'If it is!'

'It is.'

'What if it is not?'

***

What a fool I was. There they are. Both of them. The child and he. Both on the moon. See how they wink at me from of the halo. Whenever there was a blue ring around the moon, he would call out to me. A soul flew down to earth. It was born within me. And, it was a great soul. A soul is great because it is a soul. How can it not be great?

The moon did not have a halo every night.

I did not look at the moon every evening.

I did not go out every day.

The evenings passed inside closed rooms with barred

windows, bereft of the moon. Even if he were to think of me every day, the ring would not always form. It is not that easy.

Eight years have passed. Our child would have been in the fourth form now. If there had been a child.

It would have entered my womb under the halo of the moon. That was how it would come to me, if it were to come.

Had it only been eight years? Nine? Ten? Innumerable years?

When there was a blue halo around the moon, there was nothing but the blue light. I was inside the circle of light. A soul was born within me.

I took a hand mirror out of my bag and captured the reflection of the moon in it. Now the blue circle lay close to me. So close that I could stretch my hand and touch it. I did not. I had become smart. I did not try to shred the illusory veils covering reality. Suppose as I stretched my hand, it banged against the mirror... would the dream not shatter to smithereens? I did not need to touch it. It was enough to know that I could if I wanted to. The blue circle was there, captured in the mirror. So close.

Spellbound, I looked at him.

'Come, let's dance.'

'Why?'

'Are you happy?'

'Yes, very.'

'We want to dance when we are happy, do we not?'

'Yes.'

'Why don't we?'

'I don't know.'

'Then find out. We are happy. Every fibre of our bodies is singing; every nerve is throbbing; every limb is pulsating. Yet, we do not dance. Why?'

'Because...nobody does.'

'Exactly. We do not dance because nobody does. We are afraid...how can we, when no one does...what will people say? Tell me what comes to mind when I say "people", quick.'

'Go to hell,' I said and laughed.

'Don't laugh. Tell them to go to hell. Tell them we shall dance, whatever they say. Let's dance.'

We began to dance. In each other's arms, under the blue halo of the moon, to the beat of the music coming from afar.

The beat faltered. We kept on dancing.

The music stopped. We danced on—bewitched and entranced until we fell exhausted on the grass entwined together. Under the circle of the moon.

I clasped the mirror in my palm. Let the moon's reflection shake and shiver but remain within my grasp. Slowly, I began to dance to the beat of the music playing far away. Slow, slow...

'What, Mrs Goyal, what's happened?' a voice rang out.

'Sozzled, is she?' More voices cackling with rude laughter. 'Why dance alone? Give us a chance. We are all waiting.'

'Have a heart. We need partners.'

'What do you think we got the band for?'

'Come inside. We have everything. Dim lights, music, men!'

'And drinks. Our dear brothers are all soaked.'

'So are our dear sisters. These days sisters are more enterprising than brothers,' they snigger.

So many voices. Calls. Invitations.

I was in the midst of a party…

Mr and Mrs Saxena cordially invite you to cocktails and dinner.

Oh, yes. Mahesh had accepted on our behalf yesterday.

Mr and Mrs Goyal will be very glad to come… Glad indeed…one danced when one was glad…under the blue luminous aureole, in the open, enraptured. A soul was born.

I went inside, caught in the circle of public voices. Mahesh rushed towards me.

'Are you all right?' he asked anxiously and tenderly.

'There is a ring around the moon,' I said.

Mahesh took my hand in his. 'So?' he asked.

People laughed.

Mahesh's hand touched the mirror.

I snatched my hand away and put the mirror back in my bag.

Now, I was a public person.

Now, everything was all right or everything was all wrong.

'Are you not feeling well?' Mahesh asked again.

'I'm fine.'

'Then let's dance.'

'No!'

A 'no' that was a scream and quite inappropriate in that room.

So many people were dancing in the room under the dim pale light, pierced by screams of music. They danced because everyone danced. They were the symbols of the success of the party, of the gracious hospitality offered by Mr and Mrs Saxena. They danced; so we assumed they were happy. Theirs was a societal happiness.

They danced with a new partner each time, in keeping with the unspoken rules of parties. They were not there to break rules. If a few of them were to stop dancing...Mr Saxsena...Mr Goyal...all the others, all of them would stop. No one would dare dance alone.

If the beat were to falter—the tape were to malfunction or something like that—they would instantly stop dancing. The only way they could dance was in a group, to external music. Never alone, never to the rhythm within.

This was a public place. The cocktail party hosted by Mr and Mrs Saxena. They were all social animals. Mr and Mrs etc. They danced together, stopped together and changed partners together. Many chests rose and fell in unison with their breath, but not one heart dared beat on its own. It was appropriate that they danced under a pale light, as faint as the pulse of an invalid. The blue light of the moon was meaningless here.

I stood quietly in a corner and looked on.

I was in the room but free of the prison of the light and sound of their party. It was good none of them knew I held the blue halo captive in a mirror in my bag. I shall have it with me always, wherever I go.

2

'What rotten pictures,' I said.

'Nonsense, they are excellent!' he protested immediately.

'They are not. In any case, I don't see the point of your wandering around with a camera slung over your shoulder all day.'

'I like taking your pictures.'

'I am right here with you. What do you need pictures for?'

'In a photograph, you are still. You are not arguing or fighting. I like it.'

'That's a lie,' I said in Hindi. 'Why do you need to lie so much?'

'What do you mean?'

'I mean: you tell lies,' I repeated in English. 'Or don't you understand English either?'

'I understand both, thank you. What makes you think I'm lying?'

'Because you say one thing and mean another. You

take pictures of me because you want to keep them for when I am no longer with you.'

'Nonsense!'

'People who don't know how to lie should stick to the truth. All your photos are of me arguing and quarrelling; how can you say...'

'I can because I think so.'

'You think wrong or you lie. I think you lie. You take all the pictures because you know we will not be together always.'

'I know nothing of the sort.'

'You want it.'

'Blast you!'

'You believe it. Confess.'

'That's because you revel in the idea of your death. You wish for it and talk about it endlessly.'

'So?'

'So...'

'You believe I'll die soon.'

'I do not. You insist on it.'

'When I am dead, you'll be content with these.'

'Silly woman, how can a frozen moment replace life?'

'What will you do with them?'

'Keep them, what else?'

'A pile of rotten photos to feed white ants? Lovely.'

'Stop it. They are not rotten.'

'They are. Rotten. Rotten. Rotten.'

'Good. Be dogmatic. Repeat yourself. That's the only way to make people believe a lie.'

'A lie is easy to believe. It's the truth that has to be repeated.'

'Let's not argue. I know the pictures are good.'

'They are not.'

'Fine then, tear them up.'

'Is that a challenge?'

'Aha! Now you dither.'

I picked the top one from the pile and carefully, deliberately, tore it through the middle, slashing my face in two. It stared at me from two different directions, looking more like me than ever before. My picture and I both split in two. Torn asunder, waiting to be rejoined, but afraid. To be irrevocably joined was frightening. The moment one was unified completely with another, it was like being submerged, dismembered, ceasing to be. There was comfort in duality. At least I am, such as I am, in dispute with myself. The moment I denied a part and joined both to become one, I would cease to be myself. The torn picture stared at me, a testimony to my predicament.

I picked it up to tear it again. My eyes fell on him. His face looked split too. A jagged line of pain ran from head to chin. Like an image in a cracked mirror.

I tore it quickly and threw the pieces down in front of him.

He would pull me to him surely...snatch the rest of the photos from me...shout to stop me. He would certainly take my face in his hands and hold it close to his. The touch of his fragmented face would make mine whole, joined by a common sorrow.

He did nothing.

Slash. I tore the second one.

Slit. Third...fourth...fifth...

His face registered each blow. The jagged lines of pain grew and grew. I trembled with brutal pleasure.

Tenth...eleventh...twelfth...

He remained silent. I tore the photographs one by one and threw the pieces before him. My dismembered face stared at him. His eyes grew moist but he did not stop me.

How many did I maim...thirty...forty...more?

The torn pieces made a bigger pile than the photos had. They lay helter-skelter like wood on a funeral pyre. Large and small pieces. One upon another.

I sprang at him and held him close to me, so tight that his breath, caught in his chest came out in a slow whistle.

I began to cry.

'Why did you let me tear them?' I groaned.

He said nothing. Two drops wet my head.

I stared at him, dazed. The tears flowed unchecked from his eyes.

I could not cry.

So he could weep.

I looked on...

At last, he smiled. Softly. Without trying to hide the pain that streaked his face.

'The best thing is, it feels good even when I hurt you.'

'No, the best thing is that you can hurt me. No one could in the last thirty-six years. You can, only too well.'

So well that you smiled while you wept? Why did you weep? I wanted to ask him. So much pain...for a few pieces of paper? Or was it for my face? The waste of time and effort? No, it had to be something more.

'You know what I saw just now,' he said softly. 'Your death.'

I had my answer.

3

Whenever I look at the mirror these days, I can't help wonder, was it really me?

I scrutinise my face again under the light.

A single ray of light was enough to make my eyes shine, as if a lamp burnt within. I told myself it was nothing. I was playing a French Countess in a play; that was all. Her vivacity had taken hold of me. I had grown up with the belief that French women were the ultimate in sorcery. Did I not always live the roles I played, forgetting that I had a separate identity? They had a name for such foolishness: did they call it method acting? I wouldn't know. I didn't go to acting school. I was one of those who was always acting. I did not need a stage.

Never mind the stage; I could not even read a book without imagining myself to be all the characters. I had to spout each one's words as if my life depended on it. And then Fate, that bully, pushed a daft person like me on a real stage!

A new dimension was added recently. I could no longer act without a stage. This had never happened before. Words seemed to slip off my tongue as if they had nothing to do with my brain. Why think, when the part was learnt by heart? No wonder I could hardly recognise myself in the mirror.

Take that day. They had arranged the rehearsal in the morning instead of the evening. That meant it must have been Sunday. Ten a.m. on a December day oozing sunlight.

I firmly believe—have come to believe since that day—the sun shines extra bright on Sundays. I suppose it is no fun shining on people filled with the ennui of daily routine, pretending to be in a hurry to get to work. Sheer waste, really, throwing all that lovely sunshine on an organised army of ants. The sun has to come out every day—poor thing, who can escape destiny? Its heart is not in this daily routine. It waits for Sunday. On Sunday, sunshine is a coquette.

The sun seems to be on the side of dreamers. A loafer had been put in the sky. With what abandon it fell on sleepy heads on Sundays. That is one thing about misers. They do not often give, but when they do, they brook no half measures.

I had reached the hall before ten that day. It was no strain. The rehearsals were part of rest, relaxation and fun for me, not work. Was it because of him?

When I reached the hall, I found quite a few people there, all gathered outside the gate, basking in the sun… or waiting for someone? Each waiting for his own. Whom was he waiting for? Perhaps, they had gone outside to wait for the sun to come out. When it did, they stayed on to enjoy it…still waiting. Was it for the sunshine to last or for something else?

What was he waiting for?

A couple of steps brought me across them. I saw him first…rather, I saw only him. Like a lone light in the darkness. It was the first time I had seen him in daylight. Until then, it had always been in the receding dusk or the gathering darkness. The rehearsals usually lasted until eight or nine at night.

I saw that he was not white but bronze. Tan is how the Europeans would perhaps describe it. His eyes were not brown but green, grape green. No, not green really. Perhaps they were brown. What made them different was that a green flame leapt out from the earthy brown, ever so often.

Have you seen a flame? The flame of a candle? It looks amber from a distance, but there is a quiescent blue flame within. A green radiance spurted out of the brown of his eyes in the same way.

Amber flame…amber flame! The phrase kept ringing in my ears. Did anything like that exist? I had always believed his wavy mop of hair was auburn. Actually, it was bronze too. Like a beach glinting under the midday sun.

I kept my gaze fixed on him. Slowly, the shadows around him melted. It felt like he was standing alone on a deserted island in the middle of a turbulent sea.

'How handsome you look by day,' I said in a rush. 'So far I have always seen you at night.'

Something whistled past me. I realised it was the surprised release of the combined breaths of those around us. The shadows had frozen into statues. There was dead silence. I realised my words could be misconstrued. Of course, I was not to blame. I had not meant to say anything. Words had tripped off my tongue like a ray of light from the sun.

I blushed.

He smiled, bowed low and said, 'Your servant, Comtesse. I'll try my best to look just as handsome at night.'

A synchronous guffaw answered him. The frozen shadows dissolved into laughter. The atmosphere changed. The sunshine grew brighter.

I laughed. He had made me a French Countess. I could say what I liked. My fellow actors would not be shocked.

We went to the hall for the rehearsal. There was a full-length mirror at the entrance. One had to look at oneself in it, *naturellement*. I bowed low before it and said, 'Your servant, Comtesse...'

I heard him chuckle behind me. 'The rest on the stage, Comtesse,' he said.

I did not even blush.

That day turned into today. It always did.

I did not know what possessed me but as I passed the full-length mirror today, I paused and with a shrug loosened my long black hair. It fell over my back. I was quite cruel with my hair, the way I squeezed the long heavy strands into a tight high bun. Today, for no rhyme or reason, I could not bear the weight of my bun. I pulled out the half dozen pins that held it together and threw them out of the window. Then a shake, just one toss of the head and the hillock of hair collapsed down my back. I stared at myself in the mirror. No, I did not look like a French Countess, not at all. All I must have looked like was me but...why had I never looked quite like this before?

'The Rock of Gibraltar has erupted,' I heard a voice behind me.

I turned around.

'Did you address me?' I asked icily.

'No, myself. I was wondering how the Rock of Gibraltar could erupt—it was not a volcano.'

'I don't understand.'

'Have you ever seen yourself with your hair up?'

'I do, every day.'

'Did. How could you forget? It's loose now.'

I turned around and looked at myself in the mirror, enchanted.

'You look like the Rock of Gibraltar with your hair up,' I heard him say.

'What do you mean?' I asked with a scowl.

'Don't be angry. I respect the rock. It is meant to be respected. But don't you think the shape is more suitable for a rock than a woman?'

I gazed steadily at him.

'The Rock of Gibraltar is not a volcano,' he said, but with less conviction.

I did not blink.

'Don't look at me like that,' he said.

'Why?' I said, still not blinking.

'Something might happen.'

'What?'

'Anything!'

I did not lower my eyes.

A pair of scissors flashed through the air and the right side of my hair lay on the floor.

He stood petrified, looking at it. The scissors still shone between us. My eyes remained fixed on him. I felt numb. The first thing I said was quite irrelevant.

'Do you keep those scissors with you all the time?'

'No...I was getting the properties together...' he stammered.

My gaze travelled from the scissors to the hair

on the floor and back to the short locks on my right shoulder. My numb body shook with rage.

My carefully preserved Indianness!

I lunged at him like a raven, grabbed him by both shoulders and said sharply, 'How dare you cut my hair?'

He looked prostrate, gave an apologetic shrug and mumbled, 'I don't know…it happened…you were looking at me…'

'So?'

'You wouldn't stop.'

'So?'

He shrugged again. The scissors flashed.

'What am I to do?' My voice grew husky then broke.

'There's no help now except…shall I cut the other side too?' he asked kindly.

I began to weep.

I screamed, 'How dare you!'

He pulled me to him. Kissed me on the head and said, 'Do not cry, little girl, I'll take you to the best hairdresser in Calcutta. You'll look so beautiful…more than before…like a fairy princess…'

'What if I don't?' I sobbed.

'You may have my head.'

I stopped crying.

'I promise you, I shall cut off my head myself. Don't cry. Please.'

I laughed.

'Who will decide whether I look beautiful or not?'

'I will.'

I snorted.

'Anybody then,' he recanted. 'Anybody at all. But please...don't start crying again.'

I took the hair off my left shoulder and spread it before him.

Things have become worse than before. Now when I see myself in the mirror with my short hair, I quite forget this too has to be done. I mean hiding what one truly feels. As for saying things one does not mean, they say that is another name for life. Maybe it is. What can I do if I just cannot remember it?

4

The rehearsal was on.

'Read your lines,' someone said.

'If you reject my love, I would have to go to Africa and hunt rhinos,' an actor intoned.

I burst out laughing.

'The English are the darnedest race in the world,' I said.

'Don't look at me,' he blurted. 'I am Scottish.'

'Are they not English?' I wondered aloud. He was white, was he not?

'Have you read the history of Scotland?'

'Perhaps…' I muttered. 'Oh yes, there was a Mary, Queen of Scots.'

'Exactly,' he was enthusiastic. 'Queen Elizabeth, who was true-blue English, had her beheaded.'

'So?'

'That's it.'

How did that make the Scottish not English? I recalled an English king called Charles I beheaded by his own Parliament. Did that make him not English? What about James I, who, after all the heads had been cut off, became King of both England and Scotland? The English were crazy. I chuckled but kept my doubts to myself. It was easy to forget history with his green-brown eyes sparkling at me.

'Don't the Scots go to Africa to hunt rhinos when spurned in love?'

'Never.'

'What do they do? Play bagpipes in kilts?' A scene from a movie came to me.

'Why not?'

'On being spurned in love?'

'Ugh. Sounds awful. Bagpipes are for other seasons.'

'So tell me, what do they do on being rejected?'

'Climb the Cairngorm and jump off.' He sounded angry.

'Cairngorm...a mountain?'

'Yes.'

'Is it high?'

'Enough to get killed.'

'You've been up it?'

'I am alive, am I not?' He was angrier.

Why was he so annoyed?

'What I asked was, have you been up, not down?'

He laughed with such abandon that it left me rather breathless.

'And I'm not going to,' he grew stern. 'Don't think I'll jump off the mountain for you. I do not believe in suicide.'

'For me...?' Was I confused!

'No chance of being spurned, fine. Read your lines.'

I did not have to look at the script for that.

'Why, you remember all of it!' he said in amazement.

'My problem is forgetting, not remembering.'

Naturally, he laughed at that.

Perhaps that was our first meeting.

Sometimes the greatest truth is uttered in jest, is it not? That thought came to me much later. We always think later, after experiencing the truth.

'You must visit Glasgow once,' he said.

No, that came much later, after I came to know him and Glasgow well from his accounts.

'Why Glasgow?' I asked him.

No, that was earlier, our second meeting, I think.

'For the mountains.'

'Are they high?'

'Not as tall as the Himalayas.'

'But good enough for dying.' I laughed as I said that.

'Can't you die on the plains?'

'No. I'd die on the mountains.'

'Fine,' he said patronisingly. 'But there's no need to go to Scotland for that. There are enough mountains in India.'

'I'll die wherever I want to. You need not bother your head about it.'

'Why do you quarrel about everything?'

'What would you have me do?'

'Love, of course.'

'So I can jump to my death when it's over.'

'Must you talk of death all the time? I told you I do not believe in suicide.'

'But I do.'

'Your belief and mine do not have to be the same.'

'Sure.'

'So you have decided to die by jumping off a mountain?'

'No. I'd poison myself up on the mountain. The only problem is how to get the poison.'

'Go to the pharmacist and ask for cyanide to kill a dog. Easy.'

'This is not Scotland. We don't kill dogs.'

'Rats then. You kill rats, I hope.'

'Yes. But then he will give me something like Tik-20.'

'Fine.'

'It tastes horrible.'

'You want the poison to be tasty?'

'Why not?'

'That's impossible. Better jump off a mountain. You can't arrange the poison.'

'Why should that worry you?'

'Very provoking,' he had said after a while.

'What's your problem now?'

'This love will have to last.'

'Have to!'

He had taken me in his arms. 'To stay alive,' he had murmured and…no that came later…much later…

I had said that he was to send me a huge purple-green orchid from Thailand as soon as he learnt of my death. 'Shouldn't be a problem for you. You're a gypsy. You could easily be in Thailand.'

'True, but will you promise to die only when I am in Thailand?'

'Idiot! Can't you go to Thailand when you hear of my death?'

'And get a free orchid from Thai Airlines. Good thinking. But what about the ticket?'

'You miser! You must be the world's worst miser.'

'You haven't met other Scots!'

'Then they are the darnedest race in the world, not the English.'

'At least they don't hunt rhinos.'

'I have no sympathy for rhinos.'

'I promise to bring you two orchids from Thailand but only if you give up talking about your death. One free from Thai Airlines. The other the most expensive I can find. Purple-green. Huge. And pricey. Even if it means starving for two days.'

'Right.'

The orchids have dried but not faded. Actually the purple-green has become sharper.

Evergreen...no...ever dry! Time has stood still... for them...for me.

He had said one thing more. He would not send me the news of his death.

I would find out on my own...but that came very much later...

5

The play was done! The festive evening over. Only a part of the night remained. Hours till the stroke of twelve.

It was fun time. Everyone connected with the play was there at the party—the director, actors, advisers and the gofers—to bid farewell to each other. Light of heart and head, we still had our costumes on.

Jamshedpur was a small town. It was likely we would run into each other during our remaining days. But there would be nothing to bind us together. I wondered if this was bothering anyone. Perhaps not, otherwise they could not have eaten, danced and talked with such gay abandon. Perhaps they were bothered. After all, I was doing the same, even though I knew it to be the last night, the last day of my life!

We were not a repertory to start on another play, as soon as one was over. All that we, members of the Jamshedpur Club, had formed was an amateur drama group. One annual play was all that we could manage. That was enough to keep us happy for the whole year.

It gave us something to talk about, something to do in our leisure hours. It was just a welcome pastime. That was all. But for me...was it only a pastime this year? How had a pastime suddenly become my whole life? Was it because of him, whom I had seen for the first time, that day, under the sun?

Tonight was the last night for me. The fairy queen did not visit the earth every evening. Not every Cinderella could turn into a princess, not forever.

The clock would strike twelve in a while and shatter the enchantment. Would my hair grow long again?

We were gathered around the swimming pool. Everyone was out to enjoy—eating, drinking, dancing and talking nineteen to the dozen. Only I was quiet.

So this is how one spent the last day of one's life.

The water of the swimming pool lay still, without life or motion. Yet one could easily mistake it for a large lake, rippling with a myriad waves in the dark of the night.

I knew what was not, was not. Illusion could not change reality. Nor could wanting, longing, yearning or silent wailing fit to break the heart.

All of them were at the bottle. The moment of scrutiny was over. Some were satisfied with the result, proud and thrilled. Others were happy that it was all over. Good or bad, it was done with. In any case, they were ready to celebrate it with a drink and more. A few more moments of fun and frolic before returning to the dreary routine. One small detour and back to the old road. Straight and narrow.

For me alone, the trial was not over. My life had refused to return to normal. Like a wild horse, it had reared up at the pull of the rein and dug its hooves in. It was not prepared to turn back but there was no road ahead, it could take.

I was dancing with him. No, I was with him. In the circle of his arms. My feet did not touch the ground. I was floating in the air, held aloft by his arms. I had a single gin.

I did not know it could be that potent!

His arms were strong and muscular. They bore my weight lightly. I was happy to give up the support of the earth to let him prop me up. His feet moved like a dancer's, keeping time with the music's rapid tempo. I could hear the beat, but I did not know the steps to match it, nor the name of the dance. My feet followed his without will or design. Did I have feet? I was flying; only he was treading the ground.

I was incapable of doing anything of my own volition. It was, after all, the last day of my life. I was conscious of only one thing as in a trance I danced in his arms in my nineteenth-century French ballgown. I knew that though I might have managed to live until that evening in the twentieth century, it was now definitely the last night of my life.

What made me think so? Was I drunk? That is what people would have said. No one would have believed that I had had a single gin, that too under duress, when they were toasting the French Countess. How was it that nothing had happened to them with all their drinking while I was blown to the last outpost of my life's journey after a single drink?

'Why do people drink so much?' I asked him.

'They want to be what they are not.'

'Do they become that after drinking?'

'They want to be, but they do not become.'

'Can they become?'

'Only if they are not.'

'I am…am I?'

'What did you drink?'

'One gin.'

'And you are beyond being on earth?'

'Will drinking help me?'

'Do you want it to help?'

'Yes, I don't want this to be the last day of my life.'

'It won't be.'

'With drinks?'

'Without too.'

'How do you know?'

'I know, that's how…'

Someone tapped him on the shoulder and he let me go. I found myself dancing in another's arms. They called this tap dancing.

Who was he, this man with whom I was dancing? He was one of the actors, but which one? The costume suggested he must have played my wicked cousin in the play. What was his name? I must have seen this unfamiliar face many times before.

It did not take him long to realise I knew nothing about dancing. How could I? When had I danced on solid ground before? His feet trampled the earth with a harsh beat I could not match. It had neither rhythm nor melody for me.

How had I suddenly acquired a pair of feet? One left foot and the other…left too? What had happened to the breeze? A while ago, it had borne me up, making me soar and fly but now I could hardly feel its touch. How had it suddenly turned so still and suffocating? Like a coffin.

'Excuse me,' I said. 'I have twisted my ankle.'

'Sorry,' he said politely. 'Let me help you to a chair.'

He did.

I was now seated in a corner. My eyes scanned the room impatiently. What were they waiting for, the breeze to start again?

Splat!

Someone had jumped in the water. At this hour? In

the dark? The few dim lights around the pool intensified the gloom rather than reducing it.

Splash!

Another body went into the water, making a very different kind of sound. The first had come as an explosion; this one suggested determined rescue.

People were screaming all over the place.

'Who is it? Who fell in? What happened? Help! Help!' They screamed and ran to the pool but stopped at the edge. Not many were prepared to jump into the cold water, at the deep end, on an icy January evening. I stood with the rest, watching from a safe distance. I could see him in the water. He dived in, fished a bundle out and slung it on his shoulder. Now he was swimming towards us. The bundle turned out to be a girl in black, so quiescent in her rescue that it seemed she had planned it. This was exactly what she had wanted and waited for.

He came out and laid her beside the pool. Someone handed him a large towel. Tenderly, he wrapped her in it, drying her wet hair.

Nobody could understand it. How had she come to fall into the pool at the deep end? It was not all that dark.

I looked at him, fascinated. How swift he had been. How sure. I saw only him. His clothes clung to his statuesque body. Once I had seen him drenched in sunshine, today in water. He certainly was handsome.

'Can't you swim?' he was asking her.

'No.'

'Then why did you jump in? Tell me, child, why did you?'

She stood up and the towel dropped. The inelegant black dress clung to her skinny body. Her short, scanty, straight hair was plastered to her scalp, making her look bald. Her horsy face seemed pitiable, peering from behind the water coursing down her head.

I stood right in front of her clad in my heavy silk ball gown. Jewels gleaming at my throat, ears, wrists and on the elaborate hairdo. Her face looked vaguely familiar. She too had acted in the play. Must have been a maid or something. Looked like it from the dress. She must have come to rehearsals every day. I must have seen her often. I could not recognise her.

He was still on his knees, at her feet, by the side of the pool.

'Tell me, child,' he asked again tenderly.

'I wanted to die,' she moaned.

'Why, little one, why did you want to die?'

His voice was full of love. His head almost touched her breasts as he held her by her shoulders.

'Tell me, child,' he said.

I could not take my eyes off him.

She spoke, rather exploded. She pointed her finger at me and pulled the trigger.

'Because she was rude to me,' she said.

'Who?' he turned around.

'She…the Countess!'

Fifty pairs of eyes turned towards me. Fifty breaths sucked in. I stood aghast as if I were, in fact, the culprit.

Had I been rude to her? When had I ever spoken to her? He got up and came to me.

'Why were you rude to her?' he asked me.

'Why was I rude to her?' I repeated like a fool.

'What happened, Mrs Goyal? What did you say to her?' someone called out.

'Poor kid. As it is she is…'

They were not sorry for her, just out to have fun. They had declared me guilty all right. Had he too?

'Why should I be rude to her?' I said again.

'Why not?' said he.

'Something must have happened.'

'Driving the poor thing round the bend.' They were still at it.

'Why should I be rude to her when I don't even like her?'

'Exactly. Why were you not rude to her?'

Everyone laughed. What did that make me, less or more guilty?

He was back in his everyday clothes after seeing her home.

We were dancing once more, next to the pool.

I was near tears.

A few minutes to midnight.

He was silent. Why was he silent?

'So you like me.' He broke the silence at last.

'How?'

'You definitely like me.'

'How...why?'

He bent to put his lips to my ear. 'You are rude to me. That's reason enough to live.'

'You too...you...too!' My tears turned into a wild beating in my heart.

'What if the play is over? You'll be seeing me.'

In a trice, the gin had turned innocuous. Who said it was the last day of my life?

'Where will you be during the vacation?'

'Delhi.'

My parents were there. I could always go there in the summer.

'Will you show me around Delhi? I didn't see much when I was there last.'

'But I'll be there only in the summer.'

'Five months to go.'

'Only five?'

'Today is the first of February.'

'Is it?'

'Yes.'

'We have to wait for five months.'

'Yes. Whenever you come to the club, you'll find me standing in a corner somewhere...I will see you come from afar...my eyes will force you to look at me. I will seek you out within the crowd in the room...you will raise your eyebrow to ask, what? I will incline my head slightly. Only you will see it. 'Nothing,' I reply without speaking, 'Nothing new...I am looking at you... seeing you, that's all...you will lower your brow and become part of the crowd. I will not lose sight of you for a moment. You will be forced to look at me again and again. You will raise your brow each time and ask what? Silently I will say...you, only you...I see you...I see only you. Call it quits, right?'

'Yes.'

'Five months will bring you closer. I would have read you so much more.'

'How about some gin?'

'Why?'

'I want to see if I can get drunk on it.'

I wanted to know if another glass of gin could make me believe again that it was the last evening of my life.

'You can't,' he said, 'Not on gin.'

'Come, they're playing our waltz,' he said after a while.

'What is it called?'

'Blue Danube.'

'But that's a river.'

'Yes.'

'Where is it?'

'In Austria.'

'And I am the wind,' I said laughing.

Yes, I was the wind. I danced to his beat, unconscious of the tune or the notes. I danced, step matched with step, to the rhythm of his being.

6

'Do you believe in God?'

'Why do you think I joined the church?'

'Why did you?'

His eyes rested on my face for a long while.

In the beginning, I used to find it very hard to meet the steady gaze of his green-brown eyes. I felt as if a sword was hanging over my head, suspended by a fragile string. The slightest tap would snap the string. Yet, I could not take my eyes off the shining edge of the blade. Danger has its own fascination.

I got used to it gradually. The fascination might have made me bolder in the face of danger. I could not rid myself of the eerie feeling that he could peer into my heart and mind and read my innermost thoughts. I could hide nothing from his relentless gaze.

Dear God, protect me. The prayer of an atheist! These days, we are all atheists who suffer from a deep-rooted guilt, and are all afraid of a steadfast gaze.

'You are right,' he said after a while, 'It does not necessarily mean I believe in God.'

'No.'

'You know Brecht's parable?'

'Which one?'

'That old tale retold. A man died leaving behind three sons and eleven horses to divide between them. His will was a poser. It said, give half my horses to my eldest son, one-fourth to the second and the remaining one-sixth to the youngest son. Everyone was foxed. How to divide eleven by two, four or six for that matter? Each division left half a horse in the reckoning; and whoever heard of half a horse being any use to anyone? The village philanthropist came forward and solved the problem. He added one of his horses to the eleven. Of the twelve, six were given to the eldest; three to the second and two to the youngest son. Six and three and two made eleven. The twelfth went back to the philanthropist. This, said Brecht, was the ideal way to do good. Everyone gained and no one had to sacrifice anything. Good Samaritans can otherwise be quite a pain in the neck, self-righteous and vain, bad for the soul. I am like Brecht's good villager.'

'How?'

'What I enjoy most is travelling around the world and helping people. Now you'll agree that there is nothing more hazardous than helping people.'

'Why?'

'It does more harm than good unless it is organised properly.'

'Right.'

'The army and the church are the best organised institutions in the world, right? Now, I could not join the army because I am not interested in killing people. What did that leave?'

'The church.'

'Exactly.'

'You say that you travel around the world.'

'Yes.'

'Doing what?'

'Reforming the bastees.'

'You tell them to reform and they are reformed!'

'Something like that.'

I said nothing. His gaze held me.

'My dear sceptic, I do not reform people,' he said. 'Only the bastees, largely their organisation. We start new occupations to provide gainful work to men and women. We make them clean the surroundings by way of our fees.'

'That does not reform the people?'

'Not at all. They remain what they were before. Each the battleground for a number of devils and angels, fighting to take possession. They take turns at winning and losing. The winner lords it for a while, but the fight goes on.'

'Yet the bastee is reformed.'

'Yes. The devil in one neutralises the devil in the other.'

'You have one too?'

'What?'

'A devil.'

'A host of them. One is an incorrigible vagabond. Can't stay put anywhere. Has been all over the world, learnt six languages but not found a permanent abode.'

I knew he would not stay long in India. My heart lurched. I wanted to withdraw my eyes from his face but could not. His magnetic gaze held them. They filled with tears but I could not lower them.

'One is absolutely mad. Wants to love you all the time,' he went on, pulling me to him.

His kisses were as hard to stomach as his steady look. It's only the devil, the devil in him, my mind warned me. My tear-filled eyes blinked and two drops fell on my cheeks.

He caught my tears in his lips and put them on mine. 'You have misunderstood me,' he said. 'I love this devil.'

The salt of my tears made my tongue bitter.

'I detest clergymen,' I said.

'Good. The account balances. Love for the individual cancels out the hate for the race.'

'How easy it is for you people to cancel out human beings.'

'I don't know about us. But for me, it is human beings alone who matter in the end.'

'I hate parsons.'

'And the British?'

'I would never have married you.'

'That's a lie.'

'I would not unless you agreed to leave the church.' He did not speak.

'Would you have left the church for me?'

'No.'

'You can't give up anything for me, yet you profess to love me.'

'Love is not charity.'

'What?'

'Love does not demand giving up.'

'Polemics! Escape from responsibility.'

'Love turns into an act of charity if a sacrifice is imposed on it, especially of a vain and hypocritical kind. You would not have asked me to sacrifice anything, nor would I have done so.' He kissed me so hard that I forgot my anger for a while. That made me angrier still.

'Do you remember the Seventh Commandment, Reverend?' I said.

'Of course!'

'So?'

'I don't.'

'No?'

'Not these days, I don't.'

'And what might this be?'

'You? Being with you is like being with God.'

I covered his mouth with my hand. 'That's blasphemy!'

'It's the truth. I'm ready to declare it from the pulpit of the church.'

It was too much. I felt choked.

'Yes,' he said. 'Before God and before you...I stand naked.'

7

I had given up putting a *bindi* on my forehead those days. I had grown quite careful about my appearance. God knows how many times I looked in the mirror during the day. Patted each strand of hair into place. Judged my smile. Touched up the lipstick. Everything had to be just so.

I would waste hours trying to put on the *bindi* whenever I had to go out...You see, I wanted to put the dot right at the centre of the forehead, between the brows, in line with the tip of the nose, and I wanted it to be perfectly round. A perfect circle that perfectly matched the colour of my clothes. But my hand shook. My brows tilted and went aslant the moment I looked in the mirror. Someone stole up behind me and gathered me in his arms, crushing me to his chest. My hand lost its firm grip on the *bindi* powder. A mist rose before my eyes and...the *bindi* came out all crooked.

Damn, I had to wipe it and put it on again, again and again. How many times could one possibly fix it? Exasperated, I decided to give it all up.

I have not given up the mirror, though. In fact, I look in it all the time. I smooth my hair down, lock by lock. I can't allow it to look dishevelled. You know how one looks with hair flying around. Drunk with elation. Uncaring of the world. Self-absorbed...a complete individual.

A warm smile is equally risky. There is no danger in precise, careful, social smiles. Part the lips for a moment and clamp them shut. Public obligation over. Forget yourself for a second and the parted lips begin to tremble, the eyes shine, the teeth blaze. The public person is back to being a unique individual. No more I. I have learnt to be careful. I do not allow my smiles to get out of hand. I check them out in the hand mirror from time to time and keep things under control. Believe me the mirror is no less tricky. It reflects my face fleetingly then the half-forgotten memories take over.

Half-forgotten indeed! Don't laugh. I concede I have taken to lying these days.

'Your *bindi* is askew.'

'So?'

'I like it. You look like yourself. Do try to apply it properly one day, a perfect dot in the centre of the forehead. Let's see if that will make you look like the others.'

'Put it for me.'

'All right. Do not move. Keep absolutely still.'

'Okay.'

He took firm hold of the small bottle of the green *bindi* powder. He put a little powder on the cork and placed it on my forehead. Dead centre. He did it so carefully that his hand covered my face from the chin to the forehead. I could feel his pulse on my lips. He pressed the powder; I stayed as motionless as a mouse. I did not say a word. I only puckered my lips and kissed the pulsating wrist softly, ever so softly. Surely you can't blame me for that. It was such a slight brush, he would have hardly felt the touch. Yet a violent tremor ran through him, making him sprinkle the colour all over my face.

'What are you doing?' we said together.

He pulled me to the mirror and we burst out laughing.

He stood behind me and drew me in his arms. 'Now you look like yourself,' he said and kissed my green-splashed face. Some of the colour stuck to his chin, a little fell on his shirt...we let it be and went out to paint the town...green, shall I say?

I remember, my kurta was the brown of the earth that day and he had laughed and said, 'Your kurta does not match the colour of your face at all.'

'So?'

'And one of the buttons is gone.'

'So what?'

'Another broke earlier?'

'Maybe.'

'The button you put in its place doesn't match.'

'What do you want me to do? Get a matching button manufactured?'

'You know what a methodical person would have done? Changed all five buttons.'

'Waste of time.'

'Isn't this a waste of time, gallivanting with me?'

'Don't be crazy.'

'There are so many things you could have done instead.'

'What...?'

'You could have cooked a meal, read a book, cared for the kids, cleaned the road in front of your house and...prepared for your Masters.'

'I've got my Masters.'

'Sorry. You could have worked on your PhD, gone for an interview...'

'Learnt classical music, become the Prime Minister, written the world's greatest novel, led a revolution in my country...'

'No,' he broke in. 'Better continue with me. It's safer.'

'See!'

'Listen...don't ever change this button,'

'What's with the button?'

'You'll never change it, promise.'

'Now you are in love with it.'

'It doesn't match, you see.'

'So?'

'We don't either.'

He laughed as he said it. I was about to join him when the laughter died in our throats. Our lips trembled and we had to clench our teeth. Tears misted our eyes. We were so different. He was English, no...Scottish. I was Indian. He was a parson, I an atheist. He was married, so was I. His family was in London, mine in Delhi.

We walked on without speaking. Putting Connaught Place behind us, we went towards Feroze Shah Kotla.

'This is the Khooni Darwaza,' I pointed out.

'I know,' he said.

We were thrown further apart by the centuries that had gone before us.

We walked on. Beads of perspiration appeared on our faces, making the green run. He wiped his face with a kerchief, rubbing my mark off his chin. His white skin glowed in the dark. He glanced at me and pulled me close. He kissed me on the forehead right there on the road and said, 'But you are you.'

He wiped the smeared green from my face with his handkerchief and repeated, 'You are you.'

Soon we were laughing as before...

'Let's get tea here,' he said, pointing to a roadside shack selling sweets.

'I want to sit. I'm tired.'

'Look, they have chairs.'

We sat on the rickety tin chairs and drank hot, syrupy tea. The walls of the shack were fashioned out of old, dilapidated wooden packing cases. Adorned with garishly coloured pin-ups of the usual mix of film stars, Hindu gods and goddesses, the current Prime Minister and President, and a few others thrown in for variety.

'Who's that?' I wondered about one of them.

'Miss World.'

'In a sari?'

'Don't you know this year's Miss World is an Indian? Pretty isn't she?'

'Very.'

'Looks like you.'

'What the hell!' I was angry.

'Why are you be angry, woman? Because Miss World looks like you?'

'Why should I look like anybody?'

'Not you. She looks like you.'

'Don't hedge. It's all the same.'

If only he could look like me!

'But she lacks the greenery.'

'Come again?'

'The green *bindi* has done well. Your skin is glowing like dewdrops on the grass.'

I smiled, with my lips trembling, teeth gleaming, eyes aslant, and eyebrows awry. I laughed.

'Only you are you,' he said. 'Crooked *bindi*, mismatched buttons, and dishevelled hair…this helpless laughter!'

Eight years have gone by since then…

I no longer have the *bindi*. These days, I am extra careful about my appearance. I look like the others now, do I not?

8

'How about a drinking bout one day?' I said.

'Fine. I'll get you a bottle of Rhine wine the next time I am in Germany,' he said.

'Not that. I want to get drunk.'

'Why?'

'I want to know why people drink and what I am likely to do when drunk. But I need a proper man to do it with.'

'Who more proper than me, if by proper you mean… what do you mean?'

'Someone who does not drink himself but knows everything about alcohol. Who can tell me exactly how much and what to drink to get drunk.'

'Fine.'

'One who sees, hears and understands things without letting his imagination colour them.'

'Why?'

'I want to know what I actually do when under the influence, not what a man thinks a woman would do. I need a description, not a world view.'

'Suits me. My imagination does not work when you are with me anyway.'

'Am I that mundane?'

'No, my imagination works overtime when you are not there. When you come, I wonder, but when did she go?'

'And when I'm with you?'

'You are.'

'So?'

'I don't need imagination.'

'Is there nothing beside my being or not being?'

'I can't imagine you not being. Who wants to die?'

'Beyond my being or not being...'

'...is the visible world. It is what it is. I don't need to imagine it. You are what it is not.'

'I am what I am.'

'Yes, when you are. That's why I don't need imagination.'

'So I shall drink this afternoon...'

'In my room...at one.'

'Hope the effect wears off by the evening.'

'Why, what's in the evening?'

'I go home. Mahesh is out of town, though.'

'So go home sozzled.'

'What about you?'

'I don't drink.'

'For company's sake?'

'You wanted someone who did not drink.'

'Why don't you?'

'Because I know why people drink and also what I will do when drunk.'

'What?'

'Nothing. I have no use for it.'

'How many pegs will I need?'

'Not many if I mix rum, brandy and whisky.'

I gulped the first drink.

'Go slow,' I heard him say.

'Look at the mist outside,' I said.

'The cold brings it on,' he said.

'It's less now.'

'What?'

'The cold.'

'And the mist?'

'Denser.'

'That means you are sober.'

I quaffed the second drink.

'Take it slow,' he said again.

'Your eyebrows are too thick,' I said.

'So?'

'Like a jungle.'

'True.'

'One gets lost.'

'In the eyebrows?'

'No, in the mist.'

'My brows have mist in them?'

'Can't they?' I asked sternly.

'They can. Do they?'

'There's no call to be angry.'

'I'm not angry.'

'Not you. Your eyebrows. Never seen angry eyebrows before.'

'I apologise on behalf of my eyebrows.'

'Let me take it out.'

'What, my brow?'

'No, the mist...'

'It...gets...thicker.'

'What?'

'Mi...sht.'

'Where?'

'Outside.'

'Shall we go out?'

'No, it's December.'

'So what?'

'No time.'

'Why?'

'The new year comes.'

'So?'

'Must attend to the brows.'

'Why?'

'They are a tangle.'

'Let them be.'

'No, no...en...tangle...ment.'

'Have more.' He held out the glass.

I dipped my fingers in it and said, 'Come, let me take the knots out.'

He knelt at my feet.

I poured a few drops from the glass on my palm, wet my fingers and brushed his brows with them. I pulled at the hair in an effort to straighten it. I had to concentrate. It was not easy. Trying to take the hand straight to the brows...my, it was tough...what a fog...impossible to pierce...where were the brows in the jungle...jungle in the...mist...mist...caught in the brows...swirl...ruffle...brush them out...no use... pour out the glass...bottoms up...maybe...I...was... the jungle...

I collapsed in his lap.

I clasped my head with both my hands and gasped, 'Idiot, what have you done? My head's bursting.'

'It's what drunks would call a hangover,' he said.

'I am not drunk!'

'You were. This is scene two.'

'Headache?'

'Hangover.'

'What about intoxication?'

'That's over.'

'Over? When? I felt nothing.'

'That's the way the cookie crumbles. You feel the hangover, not the intoxication.'

'Can't one be drunk without a hangover?'

'Not with alcohol.'

'Ooh...my head!'

'Have another drink.'

'I am not in the mood for jokes!'

'That's the only way to beat a hangover. Hair of the dog.'

'No.'

'Let me press your head then.'

He held my head in both his hands and said, 'You have beautiful eyebrows. Perfectly shaped.'

'Yours are a jungle,' I laughed.

'You were straightening them before you dropped dead.'

'Your brows?'

'Yes.'

'Is that all I did when drunk?'

'Yes.

'What a waste...but they are no straighter now.'

'Tail of a dog.'

'Let me try again.'

He knelt at my feet again.

I put my lips to his chaotic eyebrows and kissed them straight. It was no use. The moment I removed my lips, they were back in a tangle.

'They are impossible.'

'I told you even alcohol cannot set them right.'

'Alcohol can set nothing right.'

'True.'

'Why do people drink?'

'To get drunk.'

'But they don't know they are drunk.'

'That's why. People think that's reality.'

'To sleep while drunk?'

'To be in a muddle before sleeping.'

'Like your eyebrows?'

'Yes.'

'What's the point of my drinking if all I do is untangle your brows?'

'Don't. Look at me. I'm drunk without drinking. The world I want is the only reality for me; the rest is a sham.'

'Deranged like your brows?'

'Yes, I am in such a tangle that even you cannot put me straight. Want to try again?'

I pressed my lips to his straggling brows...they remained awry as ever...my lips slipped...were caught in his...

'I know now why you don't drink.' I murmured.

9

'Why do you want to go to Bangladesh?' I asked him.

'Simple, people out there are in trouble. I know their language. I should go to them.'

'Aren't you afraid?'

'Sure. But then I'm afraid of you but I haven't run away from you, have I?'

'Am I the same to you as death?'

'I'm not going there to die. I told you, I don't believe in suicide.'

'Anything might happen there.'

'When the time comes, I'll be afraid and think of you. Why now?'

'What will you do there?'

'What I can. Nurse the sick. Smuggle food and medicines from across the border. If I succeed, good; if not, I can always tell them stories. I know plenty.'

'Fairy tales?'

'Yes, and tales of giants and warriors with happy endings. Man does not live by hope alone. Everyone needs stories.'

'Shall I come too?'

'Can you?'

'Why not?'

'Your husband?'

'I can also say there's a country where people are in trouble. They are our neighbours. I should go to them.'

'Will you come?'

'With you I can do anything.'

'I'll be there to start with but who knows for how long.'

I grew weak with terror. What if I were left alone in that godforsaken country? I managed a wan smile, 'We'll cross that bridge when we come to it.'

'No point in living in the future now,' he said.

I gave another wry smile. I was not in the least reassured. The papers were full of Pakistani atrocities in Bangladesh. Hardly a day went by without a new horror reported. I could scarcely hope to lead a secure and sheltered life there. I was still determined to go or...at least try to go.

I managed to convince Mahesh of the sincerity of my intentions. I was firm. I was obstinate. He had nothing to say except, 'You should do what you think is best.'

Ultimately, did I go? No.

My daughter came down with a particularly virulent attack of typhoid. He heard and said, 'You can't go.'

'I feel so frustrated,' I said.

'Never mind, I'm there.' He smiled.

'You are...going?'

'With your love and good wishes.'

He must have known exactly what I was feeling, to smile. Not with derision, he loved me too much for that, but he loved my frailty no less. To tell the truth, I had breathed normally after a long time when I heard of my child's illness. It was the easy way out, an escape from the dark prison of terror. I could run without being a deserter.

You know what a coward fears most? That others might know him to be one. The greater his cowardice, the deeper is his guilt, the more intense his agony, and the more shaming the cowardice.

My heart stopped every time I thought of going to Bangladesh but I could not refuse to go. It was one thing to be a coward, quite another to be seen as one.

It was not that I was insensitive. I felt the presence of the damned and the miserable of that land vividly. I could barely eat, drink or sleep. My feelings gnawed at me, giving me no rest or respite. Will all of us continue to live our petty lives with our eyes closed to their plight? Will no one do anything for them? Someone has to do something. Who? Dear God, surely not I.

My throat gagged as my wildly beating heart lurched up and down. My limbs went numb. Was there no other way? Why were none of the people around me bothered about it? Perhaps they needed to be told of what was happening there. Once they knew, I was sure, they could not continue to sleep soundly. At least some of them were bound to feel a twinge or two of conscience. A few might overcome their fears and there might be some crazy enough to make the ultimate sacrifice. They might be willing to stake their lives at the altar of humanity and rush to Bangladesh. They had the means and the strength, all they needed was a feeling heart. So...shall I go from house to house expounding the need to act? What if they expect me to lead them to the heart of action? Dear God, was there no way I could be spared?

I was not afraid to die, I had no fear of death. That is the honest truth. If I were placed against a wall to be shot dead, it would evoke no fear. I could bear with complete equanimity a fairly long interval between the death sentence and the exact moment of execution. It would not bother me at all...please believe me I have no need to lie.

They say it is terrifying to wait for death if we know the exact time in advance. Once the day of the guillotine is fixed or the noose, with no hope of escape or rescue, is prepared for a certain hour, we are reduced to a mass of nerves, twitching with fear and anxiety.

It was not like that with me. I was not afraid of certain annihilation, but of the unpredictability and anxiety of the long, inexact period of humiliation before death. Of watching helplessly as others suffer and knowing that nothing can be done. To crawl in the slush, take refuge in ditches, sleep in mud holes, and swallow anything in the name of food—rancid rice, bark of trees, crawling and flying insects. To stand by in impotent rage at our inadequate nursing as filth-encrusted little children with shrivelled limbs and pot bellies die in agony without food or medicine.

He had said, 'I am there', and solved all my problems. I could now stay in the secure environs of my home to nurse my sick child, while he cared for strangers in the wilds of unmapped danger. I had done enough, had I not, by letting him go? I loved him so much but I did not stop him from going. Would he have stayed if I had asked him? No matter, I would suffer as much in his absence as he would in the midst of war.

Why should I feel guilty when he was doing enough for both of us? He and I…we were one spirit, were we not? He had saved me from purgatory, from fear, cowardice and guilt. Why could I not rest in peace? Why did I have to keep thinking…if only I had gone with him?

'I am there,' he had said. 'Your love is with me.'

All I could say was, 'Take care'.

A cliché. A phrase made meaningless by repetition.

'But of course,' he said. 'I don't intend to die there.'

I covered his mouth. 'Don't say it.' He kissed my hand and laughed. 'Why not, you talk of your death all the time.'

'Death of a coward!' I muttered but he would not let me go on. His lips had sealed mine though I managed to whisper through the caress, 'I love you.'

10

A whole lifetime went by.

Years ago, he had knelt before me and said, 'I have to go tomorrow.'

'Tomorrow...?'

'Yes,' he said and buried his head in my lap.

I did not let the tears fall. I lowered my head and dried them on his thick hair.

My fingers started stroking his hair and time flowed on relentlessly to *shoonya*...to eternity...

Then it stayed its march and grew still—rendered unconscious, perhaps, by the electricity from his thick locks.

I was sitting on the sofa. He was kneeling before me. His head was in my lap.

My fingers ran through his hair. Heavy brown locks. Wave upon wave. My hand scattered them and gathered them up again. The sensation of the touch remained with me throughout. It was like a mild electric shock. Shock upon shock. The hand throbbed. The mind was lulled into tranquillity.

The waves rose and fell. Current upon current. The hair dishevelled...smoothed back again. My hand grew numb. My thoughts rode dreams. Life was running its course, unseen and unfelt. I was sinking deep into the other self within me.

My hands held a small infant. Clear complexion, grey-green eyes, hair as fine as spun silk, the colour of gold. I was rocking him in my arms. A golden smile was my reward. I pressed his cheek, soft as down, against mine. I tickled him under the chin. He crowed with delight. I touched his pink satin lips with mine. He puckered his mouth and began to suck—slurp-slurp—with gusto...once...twice...one violent pull and he looked at me agape. What happened! Poor thing. I laughed. His lips crumpled and he started crying. I gave him my breast. He clung to it for dear life. He was content...fulfilled.

I ruffled his hair in slow motion. Finely spun golden silk threads. A trance yielding peace. Immeasurable bliss.

I shampooed the gold in my hands. The surf danced on the sea. The milky froth shot from the gold of the sunrays or was it the radiance stolen from the silken strands of his hair?

I bathed the infant in a tub. He flung his hands and feet in the water to make waves. He crowed with delight as he threw it up in sprays. I was drenched with water...with love. His small pink toes. His baby fat palms. His fair cuddly body. His delighted laughing face. His soft golden hair.

The sea stretched to the horizon. A divine child played on the waves. The surf…his hair. Amber water… the expanse of his vision. I had him in my arms. Held tight to my bosom. The unbridled gallop of time. The alluring feel of his wet body…I was in *samadhi*.

Time rushed on.

A thick mop of golden hair covered his head. He shook it as he said no to almost everything suggested to him. I was afraid that the tousled silk yarn might scatter on the ground. It did not. Just lay dishevelled on his forehead. I could brush it back with my hand. I did. He flung his head back in a violent no and there it lay, all awry again. I brushed it back…

'Must you say "No" to everything?' I asked him.

'No,' he said and the hair fell on his face.

I forgot my question. I laughed, patted it back, planted kisses on his forehead and cheek…then leant forward to place my lips on his pursed mouth.

'No!' he shouted, pulled his face away and stormed out of my reach. He would be back. It is to me he would come again.

He sat drawing on a piece of paper, rapt, the pencil held carefully. There must be deep meaning in the straggling lines running across the paper. The brown of his eyes had become fuzzy. The green was enflamed by the rays of the sun. He was engrossed. It was always like that in moments of deep concentration; the green radiance shone and blazed in his eyes.

'What is this?' I asked him.

'Me.'

'You? How?'

He handed me the paper upside down. 'See my hair,' he said.

Yes, it was there, his unruly hair in waves.

'My eyes.'

The gaze was unmistakably his, intense and steadfast.

'These, my lips.'

So firm. Intent on their purpose, unyielding and sure. He was so young. I drew him to me. He stood erect, aloof. I ruffled his hair, making it fall on his forehead. I kissed it over the mop. His gaze softened but the lips remained taut. I did not dare kiss them. I took his face in my hands and showered it with benediction from loving eyes. He looked on; his lips flowered; he smiled. He planted a smacking kiss on my cheek and slipped away. My hand rose to touch the kissed cheek and stayed there. He was growing up right in front of my eyes.

My fingers had been stroking his hair incessantly.

Time was firmly clasped in my grasp...only years were passing by.

'If you were my daughter...' he said.

'You would not be my son!' I said and laughed.

'You would not let me kneel for so long. My legs are lead.'

'Can't you get up unless I tell you?'

'No, your fingers are stuck to my hair.'

'Pull them away.'

'My hair is glued to your fingers.'

'If you were my son…'

'You would not be my daughter. It would be better that way.'

'Why?'

'Don't you know?' He put his lips to my breast.

'Now I do.'

'I've come home,' he said.

'Get up, come to the sofa.'

'My feet are fine now.'

'But come…'

My fingers glided down from his hair…

…a life went by.

Twilight began to gather.

He will go back to Jamshedpur tomorrow…then one day…to London. No, I will not think of that. There were many lives to live before that. Had he not said he had come to believe in reincarnation? There was no other way.

After a while, I too will go back to Jamshedpur. The two of us will grow into strangers…Would a day come when we returned to Delhi?

'You never saw anything of Delhi!' I burst out.

'Delhi?' he said as if he had never heard the word before. He had been asleep with his lips to my breast or maybe he was just lying still with his eyes closed.

'Remember, you wanted to see Delhi?' I said.

'I saw it.'

'You've hardly been out of the room.'

'Muhammad did not go to the mountain so the mountain came to him. You are the whole of India; how can Delhi not be there? Here it is. I like it.'

'Shut up.'

'Yes, it was better before.' He took my breast back into his mouth and lay still.

Time went by. The silence grew deeper. Tomorrow inched closer.

'We could go out tomorrow,' I said.

'Umm...'

The silence continued. Time gnawed at me.

'Will you sleep like this?'

'Umm...'

And what am I to do?'

'For God's sake, hold your tongue and let me love.'

I could not keep quiet. I was in too much pain. Tomorrow was rushing towards me. Today was slipping out of my reach. I wanted to hang on, at least remain unconscious of its passage. Talking helped. I had heard that men chattered and chattered on the way to the gallows. Time sat like a rock on my chest the moment I grew silent and moved so…so…painfully forward.

'Don't try to cling to time,' he said. 'Loosen your grip on the string. Let the kite soar high in the sky. The moment will soon merge into eternity.'

I let my limbs go loose and closed my eyes. It was now in my hands to invent time…

Why be afraid…tomorrow was light years away…

11

An island in the Pacific...no...a dense jungle somewhere in the mountains of Australia...what was his name for it...the Australian bush...the sea at high tide...no... trees a hundred feet high...redwood trees...solitude and silence eternal...no...an oasis in the heart of the desert. The sea was all around...I lay entranced on the island...billowing high waves all over it...breaker upon breaker...luminous but soundless...no...there was one sound that soaked up all the others...

'Richard...Richard...'

Tall towering trees...bushes entwined in the trees... lush green grass dancing under the bushes...a variety of wildlife...a high wind blowing through the thick foliage... but not a sound to be heard...the animals unconscious... the breeze mute. One sound was there that quaffed the noise...

'Richard...Richard...'

...yes, this was the oasis in the bosom of the Sahara Desert...an infinite spread of sand...two words reverberating in it...'Manu...Richard'...a solitary island...a tiny oasis...the shade of redwood tree... tranquil calm...the Pacific Ocean...no, a garden of sand...

Japanese priests must have landscaped it. The wind blew, carrying the sand from one place to another. Day after day, the wind blew, scattering the sand and changing the patterns on it.

The wind stopped blowing. The priests saw the engraving on the sand. Abstract art in its pristine form. The expression of nature's majestic imagination.

The priests bowed low. 'We are but pygmies before you, O omniscient artist, but we have a sense of beauty. We may not possess a perfect knowledge of art, but we have an intuitive feeling for it, born out of centuries of observing its practice. Forgive us, O magnificent creator, we dare to improve upon your work. Do not mind, we would not do anything to spoil the spirit of your creation, but it seems the wind stopped a bit too soon. You would have definitely emphasised that line more and bent it to the right rather than the left. Let us finish it for you. We know the wind is a part of your omnipresence, but so are we, are we not?'

The priests kept at it the whole day. How did I know? Richard had told me.

The priests toiled without break. No slip should mar the perfection of the pattern in the desert. It became an arboretum of sand. The priests cultivated it with the wind as their medium. Or had the wind designed it with the priests as its foil? Sand emerging out of sand. Sand growing on sand. Sand blossoming as sand.

Was it an oasis or a garden of sand?

Of what use were words here? The sand was mute; the wind hushed; the priests silent...each engrossed in his work, yet caught in the same magical circle of enchantment. The eternal cosmic dance of union between man and nature.

Richard...Richard...one word rang through it all.

'You are my name. I shall make you mine by giving you my name. You will cease to be. I alone will have an identity and you shall bear its name. Even your creative faculties will be usurped by my name.'

...Someone had said that...years ago...no, he had not said it, only wanted it. An unspoken order had demanded a mute surrender every moment, every minute. Two persons with one name. Where was the scope for asking and arguing?

I did not acquiesce. I revolted against the silent hegemony.

I wanted my name. Even if it was of no value, I wanted it. I wanted freedom. I needed control over my right to surrender.

A free name...yes, I found it today. Richard... Richard...!

Not my Richard; just Richard. Perfection sculpted out of sand, music of the waves of the Pacific Ocean, the high upright tree of the Australian bush, you are Richard.

Say it once…Manu…just Manu…say it again and again. Flesh unto flesh…we are one.

We were one, but not unaware of each other. We are two, who became one of our own choice. What choice? We were one because we could not remain two. Was the pattern on the sand not made by the priest and the wind together?

We were one now at this moment…here…on the island in the Pacific…in the impenetrable bush of Australia…on the oasis in the desert…enraptured by the spirit of the abstract art carved by the wind…here in a room in the Claridges Hotel of Delhi…it had the peace of the Pacific…the solitude of the bush…the blessedness of the arbour of sand.

We were asleep in each other's arms with two words playing on our somnolent senses, Richard-Manu… Manu-Richard. His name was his; mine, mine. He did not say, you are mine. All he said was Manu…Manu…!

I did not say, my own love…all I said was Richard… Richard…

'Flesh unto flesh, we are one,' he said.

We merged into one then became two again. That moment fused into us forever. Ours till death.

'Till death do us part.'

We will stay together till death, but even if we do not…we…Richard and Manu…that moment of union will remain with us. Till death do us part.

I pushed the door open and fell into his arms crying, 'Richard-Richard.'

'Manu!' he said.

'Thank God the door was not bolted,' I said.

'Leave God out of it, thank me.'

'You knew I'd come?'

'Yes.'

'But I said…'

'And what did I say?'

'You are a tyrant.'

Last night when I left him, I told him I would be back at eleven the next morning.

We stayed apart at night and came together during the day. My family was used to my being out for most of the day on my annual visit to Delhi. I had…I used to have lot of old friends to visit but had to be back home in the evenings. My two little daughters needed me.

Last evening I had said to him, 'I'll be back tomorrow morning after eleven.'

'Suit yourself,' he had said. 'I am impatient but I can wait…impatiently.'

The phone rang early in the morning. At eight. I picked it up. It was he.

'Let's make love,' he said and disconnected.

It became impossible for me to wait.

Now it was nine and I was here...in his arms.

'Why did you not have your bath if you knew I'd come?' I asked. He sealed my lips by way of reply.

After a long while, he asked me, 'Do you still need an answer?'

His dressing gown had come open and my lips were on his chest.

'Maybe...' I said.

'Don't you know why I did not bathe?'

I knew but I wanted him to tell me.

So I said, 'No, why?'

'Don't pretend like you don't know why.'

'Know what?'

'I did not want your smell to leave me.' What could I say to that?

'Why deny that you felt the touch of my body all night. Did you not?'

'Yes,' I murmured without looking up.

Imagine, my cheeks turned pink.

'How strange,' I said, changing the topic.

'What's strange about it?'

'This...you have no hair on your chest.'

'Why is that strange?'

'The eyebrows have all of it.'

How he laughed. Laughing, he picked me up and

sat me on the bed. He bent down and kissed my feet. First the heel then each of the toes.

'Why kiss the feet?'

'You people touch feet; I kiss them.'

'Only the feet of the elders.'

'What about the youngsters? Their feet have to be kissed. But why separate the feet from the rest of the body?'

'Can't you see the difference between feet and lips?' He crushed both my feet in his hands and washed them with kisses.

'Can you?' he asked.

'Richard...Richard!' I cried as I pulled him up and said, 'Your littlest touch is...everything to me.'

'I am incomplete without you. You are the missing part I have been searching for, for years.'

'Let us be one,' I said.

'Don't close your eyes. Look at me...see, we are one.' Wide-eyed gaze. Entwined. Caught in the magic of mutual enchantment. The universe stunned. Startled into stillness...the earth shook...our steady gaze wavered...at last.

My moans turned into a wild cry as I pulled his wet face close to mine and at last closed my eyes. 'Manu-Manu!' A refrain.

'Richard-Richard,' said I. Sobbing, laughing, breaking out like the eruption of a waterfall.

'Let's go out for a week,' he said.

'Where?'

'To a lonely island in the Pacific Ocean.'

'We were there yesterday.'

'Yesterday?'

'Yes, we stayed for a week.'

'One...whole...week?'

'We went yesterday...no...week before?'

'A week...yes.'

'We stayed on the island for two days, and then went to the Australian bush...'

'How long there?'

'Two days.'

'Then...'

'Two days on an oasis in the middle of the Sahara Desert.'

'That makes only six days.'

'One day should be kept for prayer and meditation. We spent it in the sand garden of the Japanese priests.'

'I remember now. The week has gone so quickly.'

'Yes.'

'Shall we take another week?'

'Let's,' I said and put my lips to his chest. He raised my face and kissed the eyes.

'Don't close your eyes,' he said, 'Look at me...'

We glided slowly towards the Pacific Ocean.

12

'Let's go to see the Gandhi exhibition today,' he said.

'Why?'

'Did you not say one day in the week should be reserved for prayer and meditation? Today is the last day.'

'You'll pray there?'

'Yes. My credo is love for the ordinary man and inspiration from the extraordinary.'

'Are you a follower of Gandhi?'

'Yes. My ideals are Gandhi, Christ and Marx.'

'All three of them?'

'Why not?'

'Violence, non-violence, revolt, resignation—all together?'

'Parvati has two faces—Uma the beneficent and Durga the militant. You people worship both, don't you?'

'Yes.'

'Do you know who the first communist of Europe was?'

'Who?'

'Jesus Christ.'

'Why of Europe and not the world?'

'Experience has taught me never to say that. The moment one says, here is something new, one is told, wrong—it existed in India long ago. I don't want to argue the point. I'm even willing to grant that Gandhi came before Christ.'

'Some tact,' I laughed. 'No wonder Indians have been putting up with you for the last six years. How long do you stay each time?'

'Anywhere between fifteen days to four months. This was my longest, eight months.'

'And they allow you to come back every year. You must be really smart.'

'I am.'

'Tell me, why do you say Christ was the first communist? Is it because he advocated equality?'

'He said it is easier for a camel to pass through the eye of a needle than for a rich man to enter the gates of heaven. He said it is not enough to follow the Commandments. Sell all your worldly possessions and distribute the money among the poor. Only then will you reach God. Gradually, the rich distorted the face of Christ. They superimposed the image of their friend and helper on it. The time has now come when the poor should tear away the mask and reveal his real face. That is what Gandhi preached. The real Christ is a friend of the disinherited of the earth, those whom Marx called the have-nots. They can always depend on his support in their fight.'

'But did Christ preach revolt?'

'He did. He said...do not think I come only with peace to the earth. I have come with a sword for the disinherited of the earth to regain what they have lost.'

'Christ had two faces too—benevolent and militant.'

'Which face do you like best?'

'Whose? Yours?'

'We are talking of Gandhi and Christ.'

'But you have two faces and I love both of them.'

'Let's get back to Gandhi.'

'He had only one face, benevolent.'

'He was a symbol of the beneficent Parvati, though both he and Marx were equally wary of the onslaught of mechanisation under capitalism and both were searching for a way out. For Marx, there was no turning back, no way to escape the logic of history. The sway of capitalism and the exploitation of the proletariat were as much a part of the inexorable march of history as its violent overthrow and establishment of communism. Gandhi was more optimistic. He thought one could escape being swallowed by the monster of capitalism by choosing small-scale industry and agriculture.'

'Strange is the monster of capitalism and technology.

It gains in strength each time it falls to the ground. Its prisoners writhe in captivity, but instead of trying to escape, secure themselves more firmly in its grasp. How can they revolt when they are fast becoming part of the monster? Centuries pass, half-baked revolts occur, the monster falls only to rise again with redoubled strength. The revolution keeps getting postponed, exploitation increases, equality remains a mirage.'

'Can we not take a different road before the vicious circle begins? Can we prevent Frankenstein's monster from emerging in the first place?'

'Can we?' I asked.

'Don't you feel, upon reflection, that the real rebel was Gandhi, not Marx? He was teaching us to revolt against our historical destiny, to vanquish a monstrous process with the help of God. He had faith in the exploited and hope in his heart. Marx was a fatalist and a pessimist. He looked at history as the inexorable working of a dialectic that was impossible to escape. The Western world today is in its grip. We need Marx or the militant Christ, but India can still escape it. Why can't you be satisfied with Gandhi?'

'We could have...once. It is too late now. We too have surrendered to the dialectics of history.'

'Perhaps you are right.' He was sad.

'What do you want to see in the Gandhi exhibition?' I asked after a while.

'Cartoons,' he said.

'Come again?'

'The cartoons of his day.'

'What for?'

'If you want to know if an exploited race is dead or alive and if alive, how soon it is likely to rebel against the exploiter, see the cartoons made by it.'

'The Indian race has always been alive.'

'The cartoons will be excellent then. Let's go.'

We were there.

'Let's ask for the way to the exhibition,' he said.

'Why? There's the arrow…to Gandhi Darshan.'

'This is not my first time in India. Experience has taught me never to follow an arrow. It is bound to lead to a dead end.'

'That's what I call an imperialist mentality. Prejudice, distortion and injustice!'

'What happened, love?'

'I'm going toward the arrow. You want to come?'

'With you, sure. Hail the dead end.'

We started walking in the direction the arrow pointed out. The tar road turned out to be quite long. It ended in an uneven patch of grass. A narrow path ran through it. Without a moment's hesitation, he started on it. It took me a while to follow him. The path ended soon and we were face to face with a rocky platform piled high with broken bottles and garbage.

Right behind it was a six-foot wall studded with splinters of glass for extra security.

'The dead end,' he said. 'Hark, the soul of art beckons to star-crossed lovers. Allow me to recite Eliot's "Wasteland" to you.'

'Stop talking like the *Times Literary Supplement*. Getting lost is not such a tragedy.'

'Who's lost? I have come to the place you wanted me to reach. Let's sit here and weep over our fate.'

'Why would you weep?' I was angry. 'This is not your fate or your country. Go find a way out. You were right. This is what happens in backward countries.'

'Don't mock me.'

'Why, are you God that one cannot mock you?'

'You mean you never laugh at God?'

'I do. God needs it. Unless people make fun of him without reservation, how can he come down to earth?'

'What if he does?'

'He will appear as Gandhi, Christ or Marx and we will…'

'Laugh at him.'

'Yes. So he can lead the people and not play God.'

'Good. Let's laugh at ourselves.'

'Back on the footpath?'

We started back. 'Why did you take this path? It clearly led to a dead end,' I asked.

'That's why,' he pulled me to him and kissed me.

'One need not stop exploring just because some paths lead to dead ends.'

'But we have to go back.'

'We will. Not even God can forsake the world.'

'The world can...' I began sternly.

'Go to blazes and take all that it might ever think with it. We will still not forsake it.'

'No?'

'No. The path goes on. Keep looking for the way.'

13

I raised myself on my elbow, nestled my cheek in my palm and fixed my gaze on him. He was fast asleep. I loved to feast my eyes on his sleeping face.

The beauty of his face made me want to cry.

It was free of all its wrinkles. He was fulfilled, at peace…or was it because he was at peace that he looked fulfilled? The fading light of the evening filled the room with shadows but there were none on his face. Not one speck.

The fading light and the growing darkness played a game of hide-and-seek that made the soft radiance of the room flicker now and then. His body alone was at rest, without a tremor.

He lay covered to the neck with a white sheet. The face was uncovered and shone golden in the gathering shadow of the night. His eyes were closed, he was asleep.

We had turned day into night and night into…day. Had we? Did we really know when it was night and when day?

Not that we did anything much during the day. We just lay around musing about the night. It was appropriate that our day dawned in the dark of the night when the rest of the world slept, unaware of us. It was not aware of how unaware we had grown of it. It did not impinge on our thoughts. Nor did our thoughts impede its pace.

The light of the day slowly gave way to the shadows of the evening. That was how our day dawned, putting the light to shame. It paused in its onward march, stole back instead of coming on.

He lay still, a waxwork—life-like but motionless. I could hear my inhalations marking the passage of time. My body did not move. The stillness of my form made me doubt if I was alive. I watched him steadily, counting each breath as I waited for the moment when he would open his eyes to look at me. Indescribable was the joy of it.

A dapple of grey darkness was forcing its way into the room.

I could have switched on the light but I did not want to take my eyes off his face even for a moment.

He was asleep.

He continued to sleep.

Something strange was happening in front of my cycs. Thc goldcn radiancc of his facc was turning into pale ivory...slowly his lips turned blue...purple circles grew under the closed lids of his eyes...

I looked on...

Innumerable orchids covered the white sheet on his body, multiplying until the sheet could no longer be seen. The net of purple and ivory orchids gathered him in its embrace. The sides of the bed rose slowly to close around him like a box. The open lid showed the limpid transparency of his motionless face, framed by the orchids.

Long ago in Jamshedpur, I had told him, 'When you die, I'll cover your coffin with orchids.'

'That would be worth dying for. But where will you get the orchids?' he had asked.

'From Sikkim.'

'You'll go to Sikkim for that?'

'Leaving you behind? Never.'

'But I won't be here.'

'I will bring you back to life.'

'Then the orchids will be wasted.'

'Let them.'

'When will you go to Sikkim?'

'Never.'

'You think I'll never die?'

'Not before my eyes. I'll always remember you like this...alive, vibrant, vital.'

'Such obduracy to save a few orchids.'

'Orchids don't bother me. There are plenty growing in my garden.'

'Liar!'

'Come and see. They are in full bloom these days.'

'Orchids?'

'Absolutely.'

'In your garden?'

'Correct.'

'In Jamshedpur?'

'Yes sir!'

'Indeed! They come floating on the air, I suppose.'

'No. They grow around the trunks of the three huge casuarinas I have in my garden.'

That made him think.

'Small flowers?' he asked.

'Yes.'

'Pale petals with purple-blue hearts?'

'Yes.'

'I see.' He did not sound sceptical now.

'There are hundreds of them,' I said proudly.

'What do you do to grow them?' he asked.

'Nothing. They just grow.'

'You do nothing for them?'

'No. They have always been there.'

'You mean to tell me you grow orchids in your garden in a place like Jamshedpur and don't do anything for them?' He sounded so disapproving that it unnerved me.

'What should I do?' I asked.

'You know how difficult it is to grow orchids?'

'No.'

'Then find out.'

'But what am I to do with the ones already there?'

'Let them bloom for my coffin.'

'What if you don't die?'

'Let them bloom forever.'

'Is that all?'

'What else can you do when they have already flowered?'

Yes, what can one do if the orchids insist on flowering? How did they bloom…in the gathering darkness of the room? There must be a God somewhere or…is it fate?

He lay smothered by the orchids. The colour of his face was the pale of the petals. A purple shadow darkened the closed lids. His lips steadily grew blue like the heart of the orchid. A sound of wailing rose from the four corners of the room.

Who was it that wept?

I…it was I…

…not a sound did I make.

It was the invisible that wailed, sending its echo to all the corners of the room.

Tears fell without pause from my eyes. My lips trembled. My head continued to rest on my elbow, my cheek in my palm. The flowing tears gathered in the cupped palm but no sound came from my lips. I was without words.

I gazed intently at his corpse. It was all over. It was not a wax icon, but the mortal remains of a vibrant human. Richard, my man. Richard-Richard!

He opened his eyes. The room shone with a green radiance. An amber flame leapt out of the darkness, searing me, filling me with peace.

'Good morning,' he whispered.

I continued to stare at him with tears pouring into my cupped palm.

He took my face in his hands, raised his head and drank the tears stored in my palm.

He threw his head back on the pillow and said again, 'Good morning.'

'Good morning,' I mumbled.

'Why so salty?'

'What?'

'This morning?'

He put his lips on mine. The salt made my tongue tingle. 'Isn't it?'

'Yes.'

'Why?'

'I thought you were dead.'

'Without the orchids? Never.'

'There were orchids.'

'You have brought me back to life. Why cry now?

You know I die every night and come alive every morning.'

'It's evening now,' I said.

'Good evening,' he said.

'I have to go,' I said sadly.

'Good night then.'

'Nothing more?'

'Get to work, the morning is here. We are not on our honeymoon, to spend the whole day making love.'

'How am I to spend the day?'

'Think of me.'

'That makes it a honeymoon.'

'Seems like two weeks were not enough for you.'

'Our honeymoon would last a lifetime.'

'What about work?'

'We would work when this life is over.'

'In the next birth?'

'Yes.'

'Fine. From today, I believe in rebirth.'

'Thank God. I was afraid you might go back tomorrow.'

'No, I can go back only after this life is over.'

'How long will it last?'

'Tell me.'

'Two weeks more…no please, make it four.'

'I'll stay for at least four more days.'

'I'll come tomorrow…no, tonight…good morning.'

14

'Thirty years more, then I'll be with you.'

'Only thirty?'

'What are thirty years? A few months put together.'

'Or weeks.'

'A few days in a week.'

'Or hours.'

'Minutes in each hour.'

'Or seconds.'

'They'll pass all too soon.'

'Richard-Richard, I'll say, three times in a second and it'll pass.'

'And I, Manu, four times every second and it will be gone.'

'You want to be ahead in this too?'

'Yes, your name is shorter than mine.'

'What's in a name?'

'And you are younger.'

'So?'

'I was, when you were not. You will be, when I am gone.'

'I don't want to hear that.'

'All right, but you cannot deny that you will only be sixty in thirty years while I will be sixty-five.'

'So what, sixty-five is not that old.'

'No. And sixty is really young.'

'Yes.'

'You will keep your promise, won't you?'

'Yes. No one cares what a woman of sixty does. Where will you meet me?'

'In Paris.'

'Will do.'

'It's beautiful, the city of lovers.'

'But you said you would take me to Hong Kong for our honeymoon.'

'And I will.'

'We could not go…then.'

'Yes…we were late.'

'Late?

'By ten years.'

'How ten?'

'When did I first come to India?'

'When?'

'Ten years ago. Had you met me then, I would have taken you to Hong Kong for our honeymoon.'

'Why didn't we?'

'Goodness knows where you were.'

'You did not make a proper search.'

'I did. I went to each and every city.'

'Delhi too?'

'Yes.

'How long did you stay here?'

'Two months.'

'Only two?'

'Yes.'

'When?'

'Summer.'

'Of all the seasons!'

'Why, is heaven out of bounds in summer?'

'Two months are not long enough to get there.'

'A blunder.'

'Not the only one.'

'You should have let me know.'

'What?'

'That you were in Delhi.'

'You are a nomad. How was I to know your address?'

'Just my luck. To roam around the whole world and reach Delhi in the summer, that too for two months. You are right. Two months are not enough to attain heaven. For that one needs...thirty years.'

'The ball is in my court now. I'll find you.'

'From Paris...to Hong Kong...Istanbul...Vienna... Rome...Florence...Yugoslavia...Greece...'

'So many moments, all ours!'

'Countless.'

'People are mad!'

'Why?'

'They stop gossiping about sixty-year-olds.'

'They don't know.'

'A few might.'

'Only those who have gone through it.'

'You...understand, don't you?'

'Only too well.'

'The body may age, but not the spirit. After thirty years, I'll be what I was ten years ago.'

'What you are now?'

'Without knowing, you know what I was like ten years ago and what I'll be like after thirty years. They don't, even though they have known me all along.'

'...Jenny does not.'

'...Nor does Mahesh.'

'Jenny will stop being jealous once I am sixty-five.'

'Mahesh will be at peace when I am sixty, even if he knows where I am and what I am doing. There will be nothing to stop me from coming to you.'

'Jenny says she can't allow another woman to come between us. She does not know the empty wilderness between us is full of faceless people.'

'Is she not afraid of crowds?'

'She loves crowds.'

'No one is frightened of a crowd.'

'You are right. One feels threatened by the individual.'

'People think one stops being an individual after sixty.'

'They don't know anything.'

'It's the body that grows old, not the spirit.'

'A thirty-year wait is nothing.'

'A few months, that's all.'

'Or weeks.'

'Days.'

'Or hours.'

'A few minutes.'

'Or seconds.'

'They would stop feeling threatened if we don't meet for thirty years.'

'Yes, thirty years is a long time for them.'

'Time stretches when no moment is precious.'

'For me, each minute would be precious because I'd know you are there...but listen, how will I know you are...?'

'I will be somewhere or the other.'

'Promise?'

'Yes. I'd come and renew my promise every year.'

'You will?'

'Yes, once a year.'

'How would you come from thousands of miles? Where would you be?'

'Somewhere in Europe or Asia or maybe Africa.'

'A thousand miles away at least.'

'What are a thousand miles; the sum of a number of miles, that's all.'

'Yes...a few miles only.'

'Or furlongs...'

'A couple of steps...'

'The length of an arm.'

A couple of steps...a few moments...a little distance...why was the heart wailing then...without respite?

I knew why I was not crying. Because he was not. And he was not because I was not.

A few moments, I was saying.

A couple of steps, he was saying...

The length of an arm...yet...why did every bone splinter and break under the blow?

The body was nothing but bone, flesh and skin. Blood, water and air. It was the spirit which mattered. Yet...it was the flesh that screamed...skin that shrivelled...blood that turned into water...breath that choked on itself. It was in the nature of flesh to suffer. That was how it grew old.

Thirty years. Only thirty. Then we would have our honeymoon. He would come next year. One year. Only three hundred and sixty-five days.

I shall see him after three hundred and sixty-five days, renew my pledge and hear his. And then there would be twenty-nine years left. Twenty-eight...twenty-seven...twenty-six...twenty-five...one year less each year...countless moments less to wait.

He was leaving India that day. For some place a few thousand miles away. He would be in Europe mostly, or in Africa or nearer home...sometimes...somewhere in Asia.

At last, I wept.

It was nothing; my blood had turned into water and poured out of my eyes, that was all.

15

Mahesh drained the cup of tea, lit a cigarette and said gaily, 'I have resigned.'

'You've left your job!' I was astounded.

'Yes.'

'But...why?'

'Just like that. Felt like it. Had enough of Jamshedpur.'

'Do you have something else lined up?'

'No.'

'You haven't applied anywhere?'

'No. I don't intend to do a job anymore.'

'Then...what?'

'Something of my own.'

'A factory?'

'Perhaps.'

'You would need money.'

'Yes.'

'Where would it come from?'

'The government gives loans. There is also my

provident fund. I can arrange something. If not,' he laughed softly, 'we would sell your jewellery.'

I laughed with him.

'Where do you propose to stay?'

'I don't know. First order of business: a holiday.'

'What about me?'

'Go to Delhi.'

'You would wander around the world and I'd sit in Delhi looking after your kids,' I retaliated.

Mahesh gave a startled look and said, 'If you wish, you can roam around the world, I'd look after the kids.'

'What do you know about children?'

'Nothing. That does not mean you have to know everything.'

'I am a woman.'

'So?'

'It's my job.'

'Who says so?'

'Why else did I have children?'

'You did not have them because of that.'

'Why then?'

Mahesh took a while to reply. 'When we got married,' he said, 'you were in love with me and wanted to do all that you thought an Indian wife did to make her husband happy.'

Now it was my turn to be taken aback.

He was, of course, dead serious. He never laughed

without reason, without deep meaning behind his laughter.

I was reminded of the day I had introduced him to Richard.

'Richard Hutchison,' I had said. 'My husband, Mahesh Goyal.'

Mahesh had burst out laughing.

I had been dumbfounded.

'Why laugh?' I had mumbled.

He had given his hand to Richard and said, 'I am Mahesh, Mr Hutchison. Husband is not my title.' Richard had laughed too.

'Please call me Richard,' he had said and looked at me with envy. He told me later, 'Mahesh is the only person I sympathise with, in this whole affair.'

'And you?' I asked Mahesh now. 'What did you want?'

'I did not love you,' he replied.

Ten years ago this would have devastated me. How strange that I could now accept it as a statement of fact. I had always known it. I knew when we got married that it was nothing more than a marriage of convenience for Mahesh. All the love was on my side. I had never asked him if he loved me because I was afraid, he might say no. I had quietly committed myself to giving him all that I believed an average husband wanted from his wife. A well-appointed house. Healthy and well-behaved children. An attractive, attentive and well-groomed wife. A hospitable hostess attuned to the needs of the social circle. We were soon accepted as made for each other in the small town of Gorakhpur, where he was posted then.

For eight years, I had not looked at myself or Mahesh for that matter, through my own eyes. Whichever town we went to, big or small, my vision was determined by what the average man thought the average view of society was. Even when I looked at myself in the mirror, I saw, not my face, but the image of the average woman, acceptable to society. That was the role I played through the day but…

When Mahesh returned home in the evening, my eyes fixed themselves on his face and the unasked question gnawed at me. Did he love me the way I loved him? All right, not as much, but he did love me…or did he not…not at all?

'So you know?' I asked.

'Yes.'

'Did you…then too?'

'Yes.'

'Why did you marry me?'

He was quiet for a while then asked, 'How old was I when we got married?'

'Thirty-two.'

He gave a short laugh.

'Not everyone finds love,' he said.

'But if one does?' I sounded desperate.

He looked surprised. 'Then one will,' he said.

'Suppose you had been in love with someone?'

'I would have married her.'

'What if you fall in love now?'

'With you here?'

'Yes.'

'What if I fall in love with you?' he laughed again.

'Please answer me. If you fall in love while married to me, what then?'

'If I...really do...?'

I knew he was trying hard to lie but he could not. In the last ten years, he had not lied about anything important. After a long tussle with himself, he said gently but firmly, 'I don't consider marriage ties binding, Manu.' He avoided looking at me.

'What if I fall in love?'

He did not say anything.

'Tell me, what if I am in love?'

He was silent for so long that I thought he had forgotten my question and was preoccupied with something else. After all, he had just resigned his job. There was so much to occupy him. I grew anxious. A man who could give up a prestigious and lucrative position at a moment's notice could do anything.

At last he broke his silence. 'If you do,' he said, 'try not to tell me.'

Richard had once said, 'Confession is for the cowardly.'

'But you people believe in confession,' I had objected.

'Catholics do.'

'You are Protestant?'

'Yes.'

'You don't have to confess?'

'No.'

'What would you say to Jenny?'

'Nothing.'

'Won't that be lying?'

'Perhaps. But confession would be worse. It might lighten my burden by making me feel self-righteous, that's why one confesses. Imagine what it does to the one wronged. Torn by jealousy and insecurity, would she not lose her peace of mind forever?'

'Do you feel you have sinned? Is there guilt in your heart?'

'No.'

'Why not?'

'Perhaps because you have become part of God... no...God himself for me. I am incomplete without you.'

'Isn't that a sin against God?'

'No.'

'What is sin then?'

'That which makes one feel like a sinner.'

'This is not a sin because you do not feel like a sinner?'

'Yes.'

'That means one sins against oneself, not against God?'

'Yes.'

'You are not a sinner because you chose me of your free will. Chose, as a conscious act, something that could have been a sin?'

'Yes.'

'But society considers it a sin.'

'Society is not God.'

'Nor are you.'

'I am cast in the image of God.'

'So is society. You are a part of it.'

'God created man, not society, in his image.'

'You mean man created God in his image.'

'You can say that, not I. All I know is that God determines our birth and death but not our will. The Testament says, "thou mayest."'

'You mean we act according to our will.'

'Yes.'

'You chose me of your free will?'

'Yes.'

'There's no guilt in you.'

'No.'

'Then you will be with me forever, Richard.'

Mahesh got up and came to me. He stood by me with his hand on my head so I could not see his face.

He laughed sadly but without malice.

'Manu, something strange has happened to me,' he said. 'I...when you stopped loving me, I went and fell in love with you.'

What was Mahesh saying?

Was it the truth? Perhaps it was. I had not looked at him for so long. I had regained my personal vision after I met Richard, but I had not turned it towards Mahesh. I would have known otherwise that he spoke nothing but the truth.

I...I loved Richard...only him.

I felt like falling in Mahesh's lap, clasping him to my breast and crying. What am I to do Mahesh? I love Richard...only him. He is not here...there is no way I can go to him. Still I love him...only him.

Others may not understand but Mahesh would. Had he not known, even then, at the time of our marriage and soon after, that he did not love me but I loved him? He would understand. Most definitely and that was why he could not be told.

Tears fell from my eyes into my lap as I sat erect and unmoved. I used my willpower not to double up but I could not stop the tears from falling. I pressed my lips with my palms and hoped he could not see my face just as I did not see his. His hand continued to rest on my head.

'Don't be sad,' he said. 'Perhaps two people can never love each other at the same time. When one does, the other does not and when the other does…It is my fault. I was late.'

My tears turned into a flood.

'The important thing is to love, not to be loved,' he whispered more to himself than to me.

I sat straight and silent with clenched teeth, trying to dam my tears, unsuccessfully.

He removed his hand from my head and sat beside me. He did not take the chair facing me. I knew he wanted me to pretend that he had not seen my tears. I was not to look at him until my eyes were dry.

'Tell me one thing,' he said, 'Wouldn't society find it difficult to function if all husbands and wives were madly in love with each other?'

He laughed freely now.

'If everyone gets engrossed in the business of love, who would take care of the mundane but important matters? Children would be neglected. The old and the infirm would die. Business would come to a standstill. No one would go into politics. Men and women would lie drunk with each other and the country would go to dogs. One can't think of all that when in love, can one?'

I did not say anything. My tears had stopped but I could not trust my voice.

'Our society is mature. It has found a fool proof safeguard. Arranged marriage. Right?'

'Right,' I said. My voice faltered a bit but I managed to control it. Soon I could speak normally. 'What kind of factory do you want to set up?'

'We'll see. At the moment, all I want is a hot cup of tea.'

I got up and brought him a fresh cup.

I gave him the tea and said brightly, 'We have been in Jamshedpur for too long. It'll be good to go somewhere else now.'

'Yes. We have never lived at one place for four years before.'

'Nor have we left it so suddenly.'

'A deep-rooted pole has to be pulled out quickly.'

'You mean we are free to go wherever we like.'

'Yes, where would you like to live?'

'Anywhere!' The words sprang to my lips but I pushed them back. I knew that he knew, it was all the same to me, but that could not be said.

It did not matter to me whether I lived in Jamshedpur, Gorakhpur, Kanpur, Mumbai, Chennai or Modinagar. We had been to all those places in turn. Mahesh took and left jobs just as he picked up cards and threw down his hand in a game. So far he had been lucky—the game had been his, at least the game of cards. A new place perhaps this time, Calcutta, Hyderabad, Bangalore…

'Bangalore,' I said. 'That's a nice place.'

'What's nice about it?'

'Well, open spaces, lots of flowers, good weather, the same throughout the year...neither hot nor cold.'

'It's no fun living in a place where even the weather does not change.'

'Hyderabad then?'

'Hyderabad!' he sounded contemptuous. 'What about Delhi? The weather would change all the time.'

'Yes...it...would...' I had begun to lose interest.

'How about another cup of tea?' he said.

'I'll get it,' I jumped up.

'Shall we go to Ooty?'

'Let's,' I concurred promptly.

'Where shall we go?'

'Where did you say?'

'Ooty.'

'Ooty...yes, it'll be nice to live there.'

'Not to live, for a vacation.'

'When do we go?'

'Why are you not saying no to anything?' he said so quietly, it shook me.

'Of course I am.' I took hold of myself. 'I mean... there is nothing to say no to. Now, if we go to Ooty...'

'Forget it,' he said. 'Get the tea.'

16

Mahesh came home for lunch today.

I grew alert. I watched him carefully as I served him food. He was engrossed in thought but ate slowly, chewing each morsel unhurriedly, as he always did. He never spoke while eating. He was not a great talker anyway, but fell silent when engaged in anything physical.

I watched him eat but could not fathom what exactly he intended to do afterwards.

I served him but I did not eat myself. He did not notice. It was a matter of habit. I left food uneaten so often that it escaped notice whether I had eaten or not. I could not eat when my senses were on alert. That is why my body was in a stupor most of the time. We do not live by the body alone. We have a heart and a mind. Both order the body about. The poor body stands by and waits silently as the heart and mind fight to gain suzerainty over it. When one wins, an uneasy truce ensures. The body knows whom it will have to obey that day.

Those days my body had grown lethargic, somnolent, most of the time. Yet it managed to carry out the dictates of the heart.

I sat in my room writing letters. I did not know how many I had written in the last five years.

One day someone had mistaken my poems for letters and torn them up. These letters might now be mistaken for poems, if someone cared to read them. My right hand was the energetic one. It took hold of the pen and ran fast on the paper, directed by the heart. The rest of the creature continued to sleep. I was aware of only one part of my body, the right hand. My body was fragmented; I became the part the occasion demanded.

Mahesh finished eating. I waited. Would he rest now or…it was for him to decide…

Mahesh washed his hands and face. He was ready to go. He looked alert, not tired at all.

I went to the door to see him off.

He stretched his arm to open the door then turned around to look at me, to feel my physical closeness. He pulled me to him and turned back to the door. I was thrown against his chest. His hands were free to come to my breasts. He squeezed them hard with the possessive fondness of one who believed himself to be their owner. I knew he would make love to me that night.

I started turning into an object from that moment.

Mahesh did not say anything nor did he look at me again. The pressure of his hands on my breasts eased. He let me go, opened the door and went out.

I always knew beforehand when Mahesh planned to make love to me...long experience had taught me. As soon as I realised what was happening, I began to turn into a creature of flesh.

I decided to take a bath that afternoon. I had all the time at my disposal. I did not plan to write letters that day.

I took off my clothes and scrutinised my naked body. It was still young, perhaps beautiful ...it was beautiful. The beauty of the body lay in its youth.

I began to wash it carefully. Not routine pouring of water on the shoulders. No pause in the process to reflect on the contents of the letter I would write that day. My mind was fully involved in the cleansing of my flesh. I washed my body with the same attention to detail with which Mahesh washed his car every Sunday. It had to last him a whole week. I was more ruthless. More like a nurse getting a patient ready for surgery.

I took his razor and shaved off the hair on my body.

I rubbed my feet clean with a pumice stone. The heels, soles and all the toes. They first went white then grew pink with the scrubbing. They looked like a pair of tiny robins.

I fell in love with my feet. Shyly, I touched the pink

heels, the dimpled soles, the baby soft toes, one by one.

This tickled me. I kept stroking them tenderly. The dull ache turned into undulating waves of pain that rose to a peak then subsided.

I wanted someone to smother them with his hands and kiss them.

No, I did not lose sight of my goal. I knew my body was not just my feet. There were other parts and each had its use. I left my feet to their fate.

I took each part in my hands, rubbed it mercilessly with soap and washed it...not one would escape from the attack. My mind stood resolutely on guard. Ruthless in the execution of its duty until the time came when I was reduced to nothing more than a living mound of flesh.

Mahesh's hands were kneading my breasts.

He had powerful and beautiful hands. Square, fleshy palms and the long, tapering fingers of an artist. He was an industrialist, but he could have been an artist. Had he been a sitar player, his fingers would have brought forth passionate music from the strings.

I was the instrument his fingers used for musical practice. Not I...my breasts.

Suppose the whole of my body had been a breast—an enormous, gigantic palpable boob. Round like a globe. Mahesh could have lain sprawled on it. His lips, hands and feet would have played with it, sucked and mauled and trampled it at the same time. He would have squeezed the nipple with his lips and at the same time pummelled the rest of the breast with his powerful hands. It could have borne his cruellest blow; its increased dimension would have lent it the power. It would have throbbed like a piano under his fingers. Violent, tumultuous music would have filled the room... if only I had been a massive boob! Mahesh's lips would have left mine to latch on the breast, helping his fingers to bruise it. My senses would have exploded within me. I would have moaned with passion. My passion would have touched him. His lips would have mauled the nipple, his fingers would have grown savage in their flagellation and he would have entered my body long before now...

Now his lips were on mine. He had pushed my mouth open with his tongue and taken possession. The tissues of my tongue were tingling...I was only a tongue.

...his hands were on my breasts. Two fingers formed a noose, tightened around the nipple, twisted and pulled it, and thrust it away. I understood he wanted his lips to molest it now.

He must be yearning for three pairs of lips. He could then fasten one pair to my lips and one pair on each of my breasts. He could have pulled them close to bring the nipples together and captured both with one pair of lips. He could then put the third pair on the lips between my legs that panted even then in expectation of his imminent penetration. He had only one pair of lips though and they were busy helping his tongue. Had my body been an enormous boob, he would not have been put to such inconvenience. His lips and fingers could have assaulted me at the same time. My eyes were closed but my body lay awake. It totted up each one of his touches. I could not see anything; the room was in darkness. I was grateful for that. My body was familiar with each stroke and shot of the game played on it.

To make love was a game, an art, a need, a demand of the body.

To love was…stupid?

My body was a sentient being; it perused well the elaborate engraving carved on it. Many of the flowers had been etched with its active participation. It was the fountainhead of desire…my body…it was I…

I did not know exactly when I clasped Mahesh in my arms and carved flowers of red, blue and purple on his neck and arms with my lips and tongue.

My eyes were closed. I could clearly hear, right there in my room, the tinkle of ankle bells, the beat of the tabla—a passionate rhythm. Not for a moment did the beat falter. Whenever I was with Mahesh that sound held me in thrall.

While women who sold their bodies for money

and were nothing but flesh, immersed themselves in the worship of the flesh, they worshipped music and dance too.

The body is music; dance too is the body. The body is the Lord; the invocation too is the body. The body is the spirit; its ecstasy too is the body. As long as the body is pledged, the heart and the mind grow irrelevant. It is not greedy though. As soon as it extracts its due, it lets go. Once the body pays back all its debts, every bit that is due, it will be set free. It can then go to sleep if it so wishes...till the next instalment is due.

Every part of mine was in contact with some part of Mahesh's body. My body was still fragmented but the cohesive touch of his body on mine had, for the moment, integrated it into a single whole.

What was I but a body and that too not mine but Mahesh's, his touch and his flesh...

There was no one in the room except Mahesh's body and mine, not even the light. Even if we had opened our eyes, we would have seen nothing—it was so dark. We kept them closed, afraid that the facility to see might dampen the rising tide of passion.

Mahesh entered my body. It was nothing; this intercourse between man and woman, nothing but an inherited intense longing in every man to fill a hole.

Our bodies merged and lay as one on the bed, writhing, moaning, and sweating—waiting for the currents of ecstasy to sweep over us, until the final shock left us insensible with a last shuddering cry.

Mahesh could then go to sleep and I could open my eyes after casting aside my half-asleep body.

The darkness of the room was peaceful. What of the body? It went to sleep eventually...it always did.

Let me first go to the bathroom and wash it all away. The blue marks are of no consequence, they would fade on their own in a day or two.

17

His letter will not come now. Two years have gone by. Another two will pass. Then two more...no, his letter will never come now. The realisation flared up inside me over and over again.

In the kitchen, the gas burned, the flame on high. The oil spluttered in the frying pan.

No, I will not hear of him anymore. I had no idea where he was...Bangladesh, Israel, Vietnam, Korea, Lebanon...he could be anywhere. Wherever he was needed; wherever suffering was the lot of the many, not one. I will never know where he was again. What if I do not know whether he is or...he is not?

The hot oil started smoking. I turned the flame down.

Each bone in my body sputtered. Black smoke billowed out of every nerve, burnt to a cinder. There was no way I could put that flame on low.

If only I could turn into an insect like Kafka's Gregor. No one would knock on my door or dare cross the threshold to my room. People would pass by stealthily; afraid they might have to come inside if they made any sound. They would not raise their voices above a whisper even while talking to each other. I could listen to them if I felt like, not if I did not. No one would come close to talk to me. I would lie under the sofa or in a dark corner of the room, away from the gaze of all and no one would bother to turn their eyes towards me. If only I could breed repulsion in them at first sight…I would no longer have to groom myself to look beautiful.

I had finished grating the marrow. I was mixing gram flour in it to make koftas. All my in-laws, the father and the mother, the elder and the younger brothers with their respective wives and the only sister with her husband were coming for dinner that evening. How many would that be? Eight. Plus nine children. Four of the elder brother, two of the younger and three of the sister. Then the two of us and our two girls. That made twenty-one for dinner. How many koftas would I need? Three per person…no, two would do… altogether sixty. Should I grate some more marrow? I suppose I should…add more flour too perhaps…they may break otherwise. Shall I put more or not…what if they turned hard…hmm…this much perhaps…why not fry one and see…looks all right…no, let me add a little flour…if I whip the mixture properly, the koftas will not be hard and I must add salt and goodness...I had quite forgotten the red chillies! Mahesh and the girls did not eat hot food. While my sister-in-law and her husband liked it real pungent, the younger brother-in-law and his wife not at all. If I put in too few chillies, my sister-in-law was certain to comment. Even if she did not, her husband, Sureshji, was not one to leave anything uncommented.

'Food without spices! Might as well chew grass,' he was sure to say.

If I put in a good portion, the younger brother-in-law, Sunil, was bound to have a violent attack of coughing. He would desperately try to choke back the water flowing from his eyes and nose, suck the saliva noisily back from the mouth. In a show of good manners, he would cover his huffing and puffing mouth with his hand; rub his face with a kerchief and gulp a full glass of water hastily, splashing it around. Only then would he open his mouth to screech, 'What have you done, Bhabhi? My mouth is on fire. What's the point of stuffing koftas with red chillies?'

'Chillies in the koftas?' Sureshji would say. 'Not a trace. They are totally bland.'

'No spice at all,' the sister-in-law, Sudha, would affirm.

'We are not used to such hot food,' the younger brother's wife, Kanta would pout.

'Really! You call yourself a Dilliwala! They are notorious for guzzling spices.' The elder brother's wife from Kanpur would throw down the gauntlet.

'As if Kanpurwalas are not!'

'Not like the Dilliwalas. As far as my family is concerned, we do not believe in fussing. Hot or bland, we quietly eat the food we are given. Your brother is so simple that he does not even know whether the food is salted or not, not to mention spices. Even when I ask him specifically if the salt is all right, he just says, "Fine-fine". Only when I sit down to eat I realise, goodness, forgotten to put any salt.'

Enraged by the long lecture, the younger brother's wife would remove the koftas from her husband's plate and say, 'Don't eat them, you'll fall ill. Make do with the curd.'

'As if chillies can make one ill! How do you expect to digest your food in the Delhi climate if you refuse to touch chillies? No wonder you complain of gas.'

The eight of them would then form two blocs for and against chillies. The children would keep switching loyalties from one to the other and poor Mahesh would be left to play referee like the United Nations rep!

So...should I let the chillies be...or add them in moderation, acceptable to both groups...impossible! Both would feel equally affronted. Imagine not being able to decide whether the food had chillies or not.

Shall I put none at all? The memory of Sureshji's pursed mouth made me falter. I shall put in a fair amount…let the words fly…might as well enjoy the debate.

The first of the koftas came out well browned from the pan. The second…third…fourth…fifth…sixth… splutter…splutter…splutter…the boiling oil cried out in protest. It kicked and leaped in agony but could not escape its prison. It came crashing on the koftas time and again, but that was all. The koftas were turning crisp and brown.

Suppose that the huge pan full of boiling oil were to overturn and fall on me. My burnt body would turn into a huge black boil…more repugnant than Gregor the Insect. The boil will stagger, writhe and convulse in agony for a while then grow comatose. Death of a boil. Immaterial but repulsive. Enough to drive anyone away.

Would the pan overturn? It had not so far, why would it now, with the fortieth kofta gasping in the oil. A boil bursts and dies…so does an insect. If I turned into an insect like Kafka's Gregor, I could lie undisturbed in a dark corner of my room on my spindly legs. No one would expect me to fry koftas in the kitchen or entertain guests in the living room. If one of my many legs were to so much as touch the marrow, they would throw it in the garbage. No koftas and no guests for dinner. Guests would be scarce anyway. I could lie undetected in my dark corner and slowly give up my hold on life.

Gregor had a sister who brought him food, morning and evening. No one would bring me any. Not once. Not on a single day. My value lay in my beautiful body.

Once I turned into a sore or an insect, I could proceed peacefully from the conscious to the unconscious and just as peacefully give up the body one day.

The koftas were done. Better fry onions for the gravy and add the tomatoes. Oh God, no! Not onions. Dear Mother-in-law did not touch onions, let alone eat them. The moment she enters the house, she will ask, 'You have not gone and polluted the vegetables with onions, I hope!'

No onions then. Better use cumin seeds and asafoetida for the flavouring. There I go again. How could I forget? Sureshji is taking a homoeopathic treatment; asafoetida was taboo. He would smell it from the door and explode, 'There goes my treatment. What have you done, drowned the food in asafoetida.' Make do with cumin seeds, what else. Elder brother's wife Mamta was bound to say, 'See, the koftas swim in Ganges water! Food tastes so insipid without onions, particularly koftas. Why did you have to make them of all things?'

She was right but…they were done now all sixty of them. Why did I not think of it before? I could mix breadcrumbs in the gravy to thicken it.

Sister-in-law Sudha would of course say, 'That's

what comes of following a cookbook blindly; the koftas have turned into bread pudding.'

The flavour of pure ghee rising out of the gravy filled the kitchen. Mother-in-law did not touch vegetable oil, especially in other people's homes. I buy a tin of pure ghee the day she is coming to dinner and store the rest for her next visit. I had opened a new tin today. The kitchen was full of the overpowering smell since early morning.

I felt sick and dizzy, ready to throw up all that I had eaten. I somehow managed to choke it back with clenched teeth and suffer the stench.

Did that mean I was already turning into an insect? Why was the flavour of pure ghee so repugnant to me?

Dessert now. How about a cottage cheese pudding? Easy to make…tasty too. But…mother-in-law would not approve. 'All these new-fangled recipes are beyond our comprehension,' she would say. She always used the plural on such occasions. 'Whoever heard of sweets made out of cheese in a Bania households? That is for Bengalis. If you must eat cottage cheese, fry it and put it in a curry, but a sweet…ridiculous!' Forget it. I would make the usual kheer. 'The eternal rice pudding after all the cookery classes and what not!' sister-in-law was sure to sneer. 'We have it every Sunday. I thought Bhabhi will make something new so I could take the recipe.'

Then…hmm…let me make sweet vermicelli.

Impossible. Younger brother's wife would gag on it. 'Yuck! Sickening. Just like earthworms. Horrible insects.'

I wish I could turn into an insect. Like Kafka's Gregor.

They would all feel sickened by me then. No one would come near me. I could lie in a corner of my room, lost in my thoughts, immersed in myself.

If no letter came...I would be left with nothing to do with my time. Such a lot to reflect upon; so little to do. Alone in the dark corner of my room, silent, still, meditative...in *samadhi*.

18

I stood in front of the mirror, getting my makeup on. My skin was rather pale, almost transparent in its glow. I liked to do away with the paleness when I went out to parties. This limpid paleness not only covered my face but lay deep within me. I was afraid of its transparency and did not want it to reach a point where it would bare my heart.

Mr Khosla was throwing a party tonight. He was a small industrialist and a member of the association of small-scale industrialists. He had just won a government award for optimum production. Optimum profit was more like it. Small-scale business is the in thing these days. The antidote to social guilt—small is beautiful. Run a big business and you are an exploiter; run a small one and you become a patriot. No compromising with profits, and government awards to boot. No legal requirement to have trade unions, so no hassle with workers. No one could object to the low wages paid; after all no small industrialist paid more. That was the definition of a fair wage in economic theory. If no one paid more, no one could possibly pay less. Easy lay the conscience. It was a fine life indeed.

Mr and Mrs Khosla were celebrating the award with cocktails and dinner. That was the way to keep the extra profit out of the clutches of shareholders. A few glittering parties took care of it.

Now I sat down in front of the mirror, anointing my face with the first layer of foundation cream. I had just come from the bath.

The freshly washed skin glowed; its pearly sheen hurting even my own eyes. I could imagine Mrs Khosla commenting on it, 'God, how pale you look, Mrs Goyal, better take some tonic.' It was strange how people who would never dare to call someone yellow in Hindi could merrily do so in English. An advantage of a borrowed language—nobody knew exactly what the words meant. I mixed a few drops of water in the pink foundation cream and patted it on my face. From cheek to nose. Across forehead and chin...in upward strokes. No downward strokes! You don't want wrinkles, do you? I was close to forty. Time for wrinkles. My skin was free of them so far. It stretched clear, smooth and tight, just like it had five years ago...when I knew he was there.

Done with the cream, I reached for the rouge. I dipped two of my fingers in the dark beige colour and dotted my cheeks with it. Spread it slowly from under the eyes to the edge of the ears. The contours of the cheeks soaked in the colour, making the skin glow pink.

Mrs Bhaskar was bound to say, 'This radiance comes from imported makeup. As if we can't make out. I can tell the contents of the letter just by looking at the envelope.' Mrs Kapila will laugh and say, 'Makeup can hide the colour but not the creases. You will grant that Mrs Goyal doesn't have a wrinkle on her face.'

'Must have had a facelift,' Mrs Chandra will suggest.

'How? She has never been abroad.'

'As if one can't get it in India!'

'Can one, in Delhi?'

'How do I know?' Mrs Bhaskar will turn up her wrinkled nose. 'I have no need for such things.'

'You mean you will go for it if you need it?' Mrs Kapila will be oh so sweet.

Mrs Bhaskar's anger would not allow her to say anything. She will blow out her cheeks and lock her lips together. She might hiss, 'What for? I don't have to seduce anyone.'

'How is Mr Bhaskar?' Mrs Chandra will turn all innocent and Mrs Bhaskar will be struck speechless.

Suppose oceans of billowing waves were to appear on my face...will Mahesh stop asking me to accompany him to parties?

I coated the puff with loose powder and rubbed my

face hard with it. I saw creases appear with each stroke; time etched itself on my face. The wrinkles filled me with peace. The tension that clawed at my ribs day and night seemed to slacken its grip. It somehow lessened the pain in the heart if the face was full of wrinkles and the body bowed down with debility. Not because the heart grew old but because older bodies were content to live in the past. They did not cling to the present; they closed their eyes and pushed today away from them.

There must be some way of growing old quickly. Of drowning the whole body—hands, feet and arms, stomach, back and legs—in a flood of wrinkles. Whirlpools of creases on the face. The body unfit to move much. I would then drag the old, crumpled bag of bones outside and dump it in the narrow sunny corner of the verandah.

How easy it would be then to forget the present and live in the past. As for the future…what future do wrinkles have?

The net of wrinkles will deface the natural diaphanous texture as well as the artificial blush, and no one will care to look at me. Wrinkles did not evoke sympathy or envy, only indifference. Cold indifference. Cool and comforting. I did not mind paying a small price like that for gaining blissful contentment. I will pay it…

I picked up the puff and began to apply the powder in harsh downward strokes on my face. From cheeks to neck…from forehead to chin…

If I ploughed my face cruelly every day, surely a garden of wrinkles would bloom in the next five years. They would...definitely.

I bared my lips in a broad smile after applying a few coats of powder. Pulled them as far apart as I could. No crease appeared. My lips were as tight and fleshy as ever. The broadest grin failed to carve a single wrinkle.

I licked my lips. They grew pinker. They had not turned black despite years of incarceration behind layers of lipstick. I began to shade in my upper lip with the blue-red lipstick.

The lower lip hung open, crying for mercy. There was no escape. It knew the lash of colour would render it insensible soon...knew it well.

'Why must Mrs Goyal use such dark lipstick? She is no longer a teenager,' Mrs Khosla would say.

'To hide her black lips,' Mrs Bhaskar would be ready with the answer.

'Looks good,' Mrs Kapila would say. 'Lends colour to the face. Light-coloured lipstick makes one look like a ghost.'

'Why paint them at all?' Mrs Bhaskar would lock her dry purple lips.

'What's the harm? Why don't you try it?' Mrs Kapila would suggest.

'How can she?' Mrs Chandra would not let the opportunity slip. 'Mr Bhaskar doesn't like it.'

'Really...!' Mrs Batra will stretch the word as far as it will go. 'He likes it well on others.'

'Does he?'

'Compliments Mrs Sahni all the time on her bright red lips. She paints them the colour of blood...fresh blood.'

'Blood will speak to blood.' Mrs Chandra would laugh.

Mrs Bhaskar's lips would compress into a thin line.

'He likes Mrs Goyal's lips, no less.' Mrs Batra would refuse to show mercy. 'They are pink with or without lipstick.'

Why had not my lips turned black? Black, blue or purple? Like scabs of dry blood on open wounds. Even the caustic touch of dark lipstick had failed to make them flower into sores.

I took the lower lip between my fingers and pinched it hard. It swelled and slumped to the right. I noted with satisfaction, it slowly began to turn blue.

If I crushed my lips pitilessly like that every day, they were sure to turn blue in the next five years. Blue... black...or purple...like Mrs Bhaskar's lips...wounded.

Black lips like dry scabs on a wrinkled face. No one, Bhaskar, Chandra or Batra would see anything to praise in them...maybe then Mahesh would not take me to parties.

I did not put on eye makeup. No kohl, mascara or eyeliner...nothing.

Ten years ago, I was about to use a black eyeliner when Richard snatched it and threw it out of the window.

'Why did you throw away my liner?' I had asked angrily.

'Must you put full stops and commas in your eyes?'

'What?'

'Why do you put colons; no, exclamation marks on them?'

'What's the punctuation in aid of!' I laughed.

'Why don't you let your eyes speak?'

'I'm not stopping them.'

'Don't draw lines around your eyes. It makes them look like convicts gagged with black belts.'

'The kohl, sir, makes eyes look big and round,' I said.

'Says who?'

'All the elders.'

'Not big and round, they look rigged and bound. Your elders did not want people to read the message of your eyes and suffer. That is why they advised you to gag them. Listen to me. Do not stop them. Let them speak.'

'You win.'

'What you need is a blue or green eye shadow on the lids. Your eyes will not only speak but swim and prance in shimmering water. Whoever dares to look at them will drown.'

'Enough flattery,' I had laughed, but I did as he said.

I was crazy. Ten years had gone by and I still could not stop them. 'Your days of speaking are over.' I told the eyes staring at me from the mirror and strangled them between two long lines of kohl.

If I kept on drawing furrows above and below my eyes with the same harshness every day, would the lines not go deep into the skin in a few days and two wrinkles sprout in the trenches?

They would for sure ...I won't have to wait too long...

'Come on now!' Mahesh called from outside. I took hold of myself, stopped staring at the mirror and picked up the hairbrush. It was time to go to the party. I could not spend the next five years in front of the mirror recalling the past. I had to laugh for the next six hours.

I felt so lethargic that I could not make myself get up. The brush crawled like a snail on my hair, slowly it slithered. Then something made my hands fill with energy. Full of joy, I began to wield the brush with force on my hair. There was pleasure in each stroke... the delight of hopeful release from imprisonment...I looked starry-eyed into the mirror...I could see clearly that the roots of my hair were turning grey. It was the beginning of the desired end...grey hair...black lips...

wrinkles on the neck, forehead and cheeks...all over hands, feet and arms...covering stomach, back and hips...an ocean of wrinkles...an excuse for drowning. The end of the long journey on the dark road that led nowhere.

19

I was standing outside.

The postman came and tossed the letters before me. He did not put them in the letterbox. After all, I was standing right there. The blue envelope fluttered its wings and took off, falling on the ground a little distance away from the other letters. I knew the flutter well. It was exactly the way a caged bird eager to reach the sky quivered if it sensed that the cage had opened. I took a deep breath. The tangy scent of salty sea water filled my nostrils. A piquant smell, strange, but no stranger. This had to be his letter.

I know, it was the strong breeze blowing outside, which had made the envelope fly up to me. The sour smell, neither fragrance nor odour, of seaweed and brine for which I had yearned for months, existed only in my imagination. I knew... A special smell could hardly permeate an envelope just because it had travelled across the sea. I know the greatest asset of a human being is his rationality and this reasoning faculty tells us that nothing ever happens without cause and effect. We should be proud of our rationality. As for me, I was prouder of the fact that I could instantly recognise his letter by its sound and smell. Not proud exactly. It was more a sense of reprieve. As if someone had massaged my body gently to relieve it of all tension and push it into a state of sweet somnolence.

The blue envelope lay quivering on the floor waiting for me to pick it up. I knew it would not attempt to fly any more. It would lie there flapping its wings and hoping for my caress. Poor little captive; how it strained to break free of the envelope and come to me.

Why did I not run and pick it up? Why did I not tear the outer cover and shower kisses on the letter with my eyes? You can ask because, obviously, you have never waited for anyone.

I had waited for four months, throbbing with longing every minute. How could I squander these precious life-giving moments by tearing through them in a hurry.

I will go forward slowly. Pick up the envelope in slow motion. First kiss it with my eyes, caress it with my fingers. Then...after quite a while...I will ever so carefully tear the edge stuck with gum. Patience...wait a while...I have waited for four months...do not tremble so...I will read in a while all that you have written...

The envelope came open. The letter was before me. Lines in blue ink lay scrawled across a fine, crisp, blue paper. Really Richard what horrible handwriting. I have got used to it otherwise I don't know how often I would have had to go through it to decipher anything. Would have been fun.

My eyes went from the top to the bottom, tasting each word.

Only one word was clear to me...Richard.

My eyes perused the contents again and this time I read. Manu.

'Manu-Manu-Manu!'

That was how he addressed me in each of his letters. Never dear or dearest or beloved. Only Manu-Manu-Manu...my name exploding from his throat.

Signed Richard. Just Richard. Not even 'yours'.

Richard-Richard-Richard! The music bursting forth in the final moment of ecstasy...its cry and...its fulfilment.

Now the contents. Once...twice...thrice...again... and again.

'I am waiting for the day when I will come to India... to Delhi and see you...I will take a lot of pictures this time...I am waiting...impatiently...a few days more.'

Now the envelope. That had to be read too. Where was it from this time? Lebanon. It came once in three or four months. It could be from any corner of the earth. Greece...Istanbul...Dhaka...Jerusalem...Korea... Vietnam...anywhere.

This time it was from Lebanon. Okay, so that

is where the war was. That was what he had said, wherever the army there the church. 'Wherever man is engaged in torturing and killing other men, I am, cast in the image of God.' Yes, Richard, we need someone to replace God and remind men that they alone are responsible for what they do.

When you are there, Richard, I have no need of myself.

The contents once more...I wait...when will I come to Delhi?

When Richard? When?

My wait was over...my wait began.

I will come every year, he had said before he left.

He had kept his word for five years. Twenty-five days of happiness. I was rich indeed.

You know how to live three hundred and sixty-five days in five days? You do not. I did not either. I learnt it slowly. It is an art. Would you like to learn it? Fine; fall in love with a gypsy. It will become yours. It will be painful. Three hundred and sixty days of pain. Five days of joy. The account balanced.

I had only one complaint. My five days were full of fear. What if they were the last five days? What if he were never to come again?

It was easy for someone constantly on the move to wait. What about the one fixed at one place?

Could one know the agony of the other? One who

had never stood still, never needed patience. Who went through the moments of waiting, at a run?

How could one make him understand that the sun rose in front of the same window every morning? That every day the little rabbit of sunshine hid in the corner of the same verandah, running back in fear of certain death to its cave, much before the sun sank? That the approaching darkness painted the corners of the same room black every night? The same bed that saw sobs stillborn in the throat every day?

He did not know how long three hundred and sixty-five days could be in that room, he whom the sun awakened at a different time and from a different direction each day.

I know the sun rises in the East every day. But what of a man whose window opened in a different country each time?

East-west-north-south, I was not the axis around which the wheel turned. He had a family. A wife. Three children. It came to rest next to them at the end of each journey. Five days for me and a hundred for them.

That left only two hundred and sixty days for travel. Negligible! The days ran close on each other's heels. For me...everything stayed put.

One wait ended...another began. Yet there was a difference between the two. There was the wait, inert like an old rag that was mine before the letter came, when I did not know if I was alive or not. The other wait began now, like a bird fluttering its wings, after the arrival of the letter.

Richard Richard! Manu is alive. Manu knows she is alive.

Manu can see that the cushion on the chair is yellow. The tablecloth has a peacock embroidered on it. The aroma of cumin seeds and asafoetida sautéed in ghee wafts from the kitchen. Someone is singing in the house next door. The sun is shining outside. The edge of her sari is torn. People are running on the road. Bells are ringing in the church nearby. Birds have broken into song on the solitary neem tree outside her house. A stray dog barks on the road. A sunbeam creeps into the verandah. The chrysanthemum in the earthen pot looks taller than yesterday...and all this is proof that she is alive.

She sees a film of dust on her doorstep and knows that that too is not meaningless but a manifestation of life.

She is alive and will be alive every moment until he comes.

No...she is lying.

She will start dying again after a few days of living... as the crisp fine blue paper splits into four parts with repeated perusal. Despite all her care, they will begin to crack at the edges. She will begin to wait all over again…for the letter to arrive. Dying through the days, yet forced to live because his letter will come…one day. It was sheer hell for someone fixed in space to wait in tune with the time of a man constantly on the move… patiently…impatiently…living in the past.

20

His head rested on my knees. The tear-streaked face burrowed in my lap.

I did not try to lift him up or console him. I sat unmoved. Not unmoved, stupefied.

It was all over.

An arid dust storm lashed everything in sight. What hydration could a few tears provide?

I did not weep. Not one tear appeared in my eyes.

He had not come last year. Nor had he written for the whole year.

I had heard from him only now, two lines informing me of his arrival. There he was.

I was shocked to see him. White streaks in the golden hair.

Black pouches under the eyes. A face covered with wrinkles. The body halved. Had thirty years gone by? Had he turned sixty-five?

How silly. I knew only seven years had passed. Twenty-three years remained. Twenty-three years... something to live by!

I looked at him steadily.

Thank God, I recognised him.

I was recalling my nightmare. Night after night, I woke in a cold sweat from it...

A huge room. Glitz and glitter. Neon lights all around. A naked blue dazzle. Yellow lights are kind—they do not unclothe people, they illuminate but with reserve, leaving some grey areas unlit. Those shadows are comforting. One does not feel alone as long as one has one's shadow for company. Ghosts, you know, throw no shadows. The neon light knew no shame. It was pitiless in the extinction of all shadows, revealing the body in its naked imperfection.

A glittering room. Large and crowded, crammed with naked people. Naked bodies. Naked faces. Bodies pressed against bodies. Without clothes. Under the self-centred blue glare of the neon bulbs, every deformity of the body is on display, every contour of the face carved as if with a scalpel. Cut and pared. Arranged in proper order. Fast music wailing and beating its head. Cruel and pitiless. *'Dham-dham-dham! Dhik-dhik-dhik! Dhin-dhin-dhin!'* One note rose upwards then fell to the ground but left no echo. The second note followed instantly, smothering it. There was no respite from the music, not for a moment, not for the hundredth part of a moment. The disoriented, crazed bodies danced on. Alone. Not with each other. If a dancing body bumped against another, it immediately shook itself free to dance alone. Faces that neither smile nor frown. The eyes saw, the ears heard. The music had to be obeyed. Not for a moment, not for the hundredth part of a moment could the feet fail to follow the strident notes of the merciless music. They were intent on the music. Not on the melody or the sense, only on the rhythm, on the beat. *'Dhin-dhin-dhin! Dhik-dhik-dhik! Dham-dham-dham!'* Perhaps they did not even hear it. There was a gigantic machine somewhere that made their feet dance. It set the beat and made them follow it. That was why their nerves were taut, their faces expressionless. They were robots, they had to throw their bodies about at the dictates of the master robot. They obeyed without feeling. They had to. That was their nature, to obey without asking why.

I search for him in that naked, unfeeling, despondent crowd. The faces attached to the bodies stand out under the naked blue light. I run from one glittering corner to the other. Disappointed, I crawl back from the dazzle to the glitter. I fix my eyes on each face. Bodies brush against me in passing. They evoke no feeling. The touch of a nude body holds no excitement unless the face is familiar. I know he is here, in the crowd, under the shameless light. Only I cannot recognise him. My eyesight is not weak. The faces are clear, each feature swinging before me fully exposed. Still,

I cannot recognise him. I push through the crowd of naked dancing bodies, scrutinising each face.

There...far away...a familiar face. I shove through the press of bodies crammed all over the room to run to it. I find myself next to him and the face disappears! Stunned, I glue my eyes to each passing face but fail to find him.

Richard! Why can I not recognise you? Richard!

I scream and wake up...covered with sweat.

Would this too come to pass, Richard...that one day, you would be there and I would fail to know you?

Thank God I had recognised him as soon as I saw him in the lounge of Claridges Hotel. The tailored bodies and inscrutable faces surrounding us could not have prevented me from screaming otherwise.

'Let's go to the room, now,' I said upon seeing him.

He showed no surprise as if that was what one said upon meeting someone after a gap of two years.

We were in his room.

I took his pallid face in my hands and drank it in.

'I was ill,' he said.

'Why didn't you write?'

'It was not safe.'

'Why?'

'Your government had declared an Emergency.'

'So?'

'My visa had been cancelled. I was not allowed into India.'

'Why?'

'Everyone was a spy for your government those days.'

'You could have written...'

'It might have hurt you.'

Was that all? I was so happy. 'Is that why you did not come? You should have written; I could take it. I waited and waited. Anyway, there's no problem now, the Emergency has been lifted.'

He kept quiet.

'Write now...every month.'

He did not speak.

'At least say yes.'

He was silent.

'There's something more?' I said.

'Yes.'

'Don't tell me...I don't want to know. Love me... please, just love me.'

I sat up on the bed, raised my arms, arched my body and said, 'Let's go down and eat. You have become very thin.'

'Will you fatten me in one day?' he said.

'One day?'

'Yes.'

One day! One day! The pitiless beat reverberated in the room.

'You have come for one day?'

He said nothing. His head came to rest on my knees. The tear-stained face took shelter in my lap.

I understood it was all over.

'Jenny?' I asked.

'Yes,' he said.

'What happened?'

'I lay ill in the hospital. The doctors had given up hope...I gave the key of my locker to her.'

'My letters!'

'No, your poems.'

'What else was there in the locker?'

'My will.'

'Jenny read my poems?'

'Tore them up.'

'And then?'

'She came back to the hospital...'

'Let it be. I understand.'

I did not want to hear any more. His pallid face and feeble body on the hospital bed were all I could see.

How could Jenny attack him in that condition?

She was a brave woman. Not a coward like me. It was not Richard's deathly face she saw but my youthful one. My laughter, my ecstasy, my youth. I was responsible for everything.

I was reminded of the camp set up for the refugees from Bangladesh. Richard was looking after it. He had started a Centre that taught craft to the women. Soon, they made a few items, which found a market in the nearby towns, earning a little money for the inhabitants.

There was a deaf-mute, Gangu in the camp. A young girl of sixteen or seventeen, who refused to learn. She spent all her waking hours sitting and weeping in a corner of the camp. One day, Richard took her hands in his and modelled a deer out of clay. Gangu's eyes shone; she forgot to cry. It became their daily routine. Gradually, Gangu became adept at making toys out of clay and rags. She sat alone and silent in her corner making toys. She presented every single one to Richard. She might not have if she could speak. She had no option. How else can deaf-mutes express their love?

Richard had arranged all of them in his study. He took care to dust them himself every day.

A couple of months passed. I remember the church had organised a fair. Jenny had worked hard for it. All of Gangu's toys were arranged in her stall.

'So you have decided to sell the toys?' I said to Richard.

'What toys?'

'The ones Gangu made.'

'Where are they?'

'In Jenny's stall.'

One stride took him there.

By the time I caught up with him, he had collected most of them. That is how he looks when angry, I remember thinking.

What surprised me was the gentleness with which he held the toys despite his great rage...as if he was teaching Gangu to sculpt a deer. For a moment, even Jenny was subdued.

'I thought...since they can't go to England...' she stammered.

Richard had turned into an iceberg.

'Who said so?' he asked coldly.

Jenny said nothing for a little while. 'The money would have been useful,' she muttered.

That day too, she must have seen Gangu's young and blooming face in place of Richard's glacial countenance.

Jenny was brave indeed. There was nothing she could not do.

'Jenny asked me,' Richard told me. "There was a girl called Manu in Jamshedpur?"

'"Yes," I said. That's what I must have said.'

'"I want a divorce," she said. "The children will stay with me."'

'"They are only poems," I said, "Just poems."'

'"You take me for a fool. Who keeps poems in the locker?"'

'"I do."'

'"Why?"'

'"Because I love Manu," I said and became unconscious. When I came to my senses after three days, I told her everything,' Richard said.

'Everything!'

'I was close to death. I do not remember what I had said to her. When she said later that I had told her everything, I believed her...'

Silence.

'Manu!' he said.

'Yes...?'

'I can't let the children go.'

'Jenny can let you go?'

'Yes.'

'Forever, yes. For five days out of three hundred and sixty-five, no?' I laughed.

'Don't blame her. She is five years older than me. She has always lived in fear of my leaving her for a younger woman.'

'It looks like I'll have to be sixty.' I laughed again.

'Don't laugh,' he said. 'It's horrifying.'

'More than tears?'

'Much more.'

He raised his face to look at me. I saw his eyes were wet.

'Don't pull such a long face.' I said, 'What will Jenny do with one so glum? She'll be the loser in the end.'

'She likes gloom,' he said. 'She is a thorough puritan.'

'So? I suppose I can't even write to you?'

'I can't bear to have her read your letters.'

'I won't send them to you. Just write and store

them. Imagine the pile I would have in twenty-three years. I would bring them along when I am sixty. Keep the vacation long. You will need many days to go through them.'

His head came to rest on my knees.

The wet face stayed in my lap.

'Don't let it make you unhappy,' I said. 'Isn't it enough that we could meet for eight years? Why, even the tissues of the body decay and change in eight years.'

'Nothing's changed.'

'Let's go down and eat. I want to know how well you have recovered.'

'Why don't you cry a little?'

'How, Richard? I can't.'

Tears make things so much more bearable...

My days pass in huge rooms full of the glitter and dazzle of naked blue lights with no reprieve from ear-splitting music. It never ceases, not for a second, not for the hundredth part of a second so that I may sit in a dark corner somewhere and weep.

21

'Tell me, do you find me beautiful?' I had asked him.

'Um...let me see...I'll have to look at you from a distance,' he said. 'Please walk away a little...fine... stand there.'

He made me stand at arm's length and surveyed me carefully.

'What are you staring at? Don't you find me pretty?'

He said nothing.

'The whole world thinks I'm pretty but not you.' I was angry.

'If the whole world thinks so, you must be,' he said without mockery, after careful consideration.

'Don't you have eyes?'

'I do. Okay let me try to see.'

'What were you doing until now, roasting chestnuts?'

'No, looking at you.'

'Who am I asking you to see?'

'I mean you are...you. Ugly or beautiful, who am I to say that?'

'Talk straight, will you? Leave philosophy for us Orientals. If you don't find me beautiful, say so.'

'Let me look at you bit by bit. Your hair...all over the place.'

'Forget that.'

'Looks good...shall I brush it?'

'Leave it alone.'

'Your eyes...not black...brown-black...what colour are they?'

'Fat head.'

'The luminous darkness under the lamp...what colour would that be? Large too...like almonds from Kabul...the Indian almond is not quite so big? Yes, they are beautiful at least they look beautiful in anger.'

'...'

'Your nose...'

'Shut up!'

'What's the matter?'

'I know I have an ugly nose.'

'If you know everything, why ask me?'

'Is it very bad?'

'It's like you.'

'I'm bad?'

'No, crooked. Is it written in the Constitution of your country that noses have to be straight?'

'You are never serious.'

'I am serious. I cannot imagine any other nose

on your face. If your nose changes, so will you…Your lips…'

'Yes?'

'Your lips, why, they are beautiful!'

'What's so surprising about it?'

'Nothing. I seem to recall that I found you quite beautiful when I first saw you six years ago; was it six?'

'Six years is a long time,' I sighed.

'Gradually, I forgot whether you were beautiful or not.'

'Naturally, you got confused after seeing so many women from so many countries.' I was near tears.

He burst out laughing.

'Silly girl.' He picked me up and sat down in the chair with me in his lap. 'No one confuses me except you,' he said.

'You go to so many countries, see many types of pretty women…does my face not slip from your memory?'

'No, you are different.'

'How?'

'For one thing, you look the same without or with clothes.'

'What do you mean?'

'Most women stop being interesting once they take off their clothes. You don't.'

'As if you have seen scores of them.'

'I have.'

'What!' I sprang out of his lap. 'You go around looking at naked women?'

'Language-language! Man must not allow anger to brutalise him.'

'I am a woman.'

'Sorry.'

'Don't evade the question. Do you go around the world looking at naked women?'

'That's exactly what the church pays me for!'

'How do I know what it pays you for?'

'Find out.'

'You come to Delhi once a year. How do I know what you do the rest of the time?'

'See naked women.'

'Shut up! I am leaving.'

'Put on your clothes.'

'Richard...get out!'

'Uh...all right...all right.' He looked startled but went out.

I had a good cry, then had a long soak in the bath. When I went back dressed to the room, Richard was sitting there.

'Why have you come back?'

'I have to check out the day after.'

'All right, I'll go.'

It was his room so I let him stay. I was at the door.

'Listen!' he said.

'What?'

'You are beautiful.'

'I am not interested.'

'You look beautiful from afar.'

That held me.

'What does that mean?'

'When you are close, it's not possible to judge your beauty. You are you. Six years have gone by and I have not seen you from afar.'

I was not fully pacified.

'Why do you need to remember me from far?' I said.

He looked closely at me and said, 'Had you lived in England three hundred years ago you would have been taken for a witch and burnt at the stake.'

'I look like a witch to you?'

He looked me up and down.

'You are such a little thing, suppose I put you on my knees and spank you?'

'You!' I mocked.

'Mother said never to hit a woman, whatever she might do.'

'Who's doing, you or I?'

'What have I done?'

'You go around the world...'

'What do you want? I close my eyes when I see a woman?'

'Yes.'

'What purpose will it serve? I would have seen her.'

'Why do you go to see them?'

'I don't.'

'They come to you?'

He kept quiet for a while, then muttered, 'Slapping is different, but I'm sure spanking is allowed.'

'Go read the book of rules first.'

'You are a fool,' he said. 'Surely you know that every beach in Europe is chock-full of women sunbathing. Do you want me to go to the beach with my eyes closed?'

'They lie there without any clothes?'

'Almost.'

'I am not talking of almost.'

'In Copenhagen...'

'Why do you need to go to Copenhagen?'

'I don't need to go anywhere. I go because I want to. What need have I to come to Delhi?'

'You go to Copenhagen for the same reason you come to Delhi?'

'I went to Copenhagen to collect money. If you give it, I'll take it from you.'

'Money...from the naked women of Copenhagen!'

'From the Bishop. I could hardly pass the whole evening with him. I had to see the sights.'

'Sights indeed! Why don't you say sex shows?'

'Those too.'

'Why do you have to see them?'

'I see everything in a city.'

'Why?'

'Because it's there. Why go anywhere if ...?'

'Indiscriminate wandering has made you lose your judgment about what is beautiful and what is not?'

'With you, I never had it.'

'I'm leaving,' I said and pushed the door open. He got up and banged it shut.

'You are mad,' he said. 'If I did not see a single woman in six years who could make me wonder whether you were more beautiful or she? How would I find her now?'

He clasped me by my shoulders and kissed the parting in my hair.

'I feel so frightened; suppose you do not return one year?'

'It will not be without consulting you. If ever one of us is unable to come, we would decide it together, whether we would meet again or not.'

'Right.'

'It's a promise.'

'Fine.'

He took my hair in his hands and pulled my face up.

'Never ask again if you are pretty or not,' he said.

'I won't ask you.'

'As if you care what others tell you.'

'I can always go to Copenhagen.'

'It will be useless, as it was for me. If all the women of the world took their clothes off and stood in a row, I would feel nothing but boredom. People are different only when they are dressed, their individual desires are of interest. Come, I'll take your photograph under a lamp post.'

'Why under a lamp post?'

'It is dark under the lamp...a luminous darkness.'

'So?'

'You will stand there.'

'So?'

'So the darkness will melt. I will photograph you... print it...So I can go to Copenhagen with your photo fitted inside my glasses...so...be done with so!'

We were out of the room and on the road by that time. I was about to cross the road when Richard pulled me to him and kissed me.

'What are you doing?' I said.

'Kissing you,' he said.

'On the road with so many people around.'

'What people?' he said.

'Can't you see the people milling about?'

'No. You have told me to keep my eyes closed.'

22

'If you were my wife...' he said.

'I would have loved Mahesh.'

He looked startled.

'And you would have loved Jenny.'

'Never. If you were my wife...'

'You would have roamed the world and I would have been sitting in England looking after your brats.'

'What brats?'

'The half dozen we would have had.'

'We would?'

'Absolutely! We have five now, three of yours and two of mine. If we had married, we would have had at least one more. That's a straight half dozen.'

'Suppose we take out ours...'

'Okay, I think we can leave those five alone.'

'You mean let the sixth be.'

'Listen carefully. At the moment you have three kids and I have two. Why can't you and I stay with all five of them?'

'You and I...?'

'Yes. You say that Jenny does not care for children. Mahesh cares, but does not worry about them. He knows I can look after them. So, why can't we forget about both of them and live with the five kids?'

'Sounds logical.'

'Shall we...'

'Life is never logical.'

'It is for us to decide. If we want to...'

'They won't let us.'

'Why not? Jenny finds children a hindrance to her work. She is always complaining if she did not have three kids, she could work more effectively for the church. "Three kids, and boys to boot! Sheer pandemonium. Thank goodness, they come home only during the vacation when Richard's here. He's no less of a pain. More of a brat than they are. The four of them make enough noise to rouse the dead. The house is at sixes and sevens. I am the one to suffer. What use is Richard? He spends his time gadding about. And if he happens to be home..."'

'Please!' he interjected. 'Not the entire speech. I know it by heart.'

'What's the problem then? The kids can stay with us during the vacation and leave Jenny free to do her work.'

'Why would she give up such an effective bond?'

'She wants bondage?'

'For me, yes.'

'That's why you come back each time?'

'If you were my wife...'

'You would have gallivanted around the world and I would have stayed in England bringing up your kids. One day Mahesh would have passed that way and I would have fallen in love with him. I would have left you and gone with him...don't laugh, I'm serious. Nomads know no grief.'

'What about the kids?'

'You could have brought them up. You are quite an expert. Remember how you put Parul to sleep that day?'

'Yes,' he laughed, 'we were to go somewhere?'

'To the rehearsal.'

'Ah yes, sometime in the evening.'

'At seven. Remember what Mr Don had said: "If things go on like this, we can say goodbye to the play. Today, all of you will sit with me till eight and memorise your lines. The prompter's off...remember, you have to enact the play, not the prompter...dinner is at eight, but only for those who can say their lines. The rest can starve. No one brings sandwiches. If you do, they will be impounded. The rehearsal will start promptly at nine and if anyone, one single person forgets his lines, I...I will commit suicide. You want to know how... you, Manu? Ask me! Just ask me and I would jump in the pool with you. I can't swim and will not allow you to. Is that clear? One more thing. If anyone is late... by one minute after seven, I...never mind. Perhaps it would be best if I didn't spell it out for you.'

We laughed at the memory. 'I had come to pick you up, but your little girl was refusing to go to sleep. I don't blame her, poor thing, the way you had her on your knees, whacking away.'

'I was patting her to sleep. How else do children sleep?'

'Putting a child to sleep is different from kneading dough for chapattis, my dear.'

'Not everyone can croon like you. We don't get trained raising horses the way you people do.'

'Children are like horses...they recognise voices.'

'How British! Anyone else would have said horses are like children.'

'Splitting straws aside, you grant I put her to sleep within five minutes.'

'Yes. The weepy way you were crooning, I was afraid I might go to sleep.'

'If you were my wife, that's how I would have put you to sleep.'

'You would have been out in the world and I would have been sitting in England looking after your brats.'

'Why this obsession with brats? We need not have had them. We could both be out in the world.'

'Why do you have them now?'

'They are Jenny's too.'

'But she does not care for kids.'

'She may not care for their company but she wanted them.'

'Why?'

'Because everyone else had them. It seemed the proper thing to do. You have them too.'

'I took a conscious decision to have them.'

'Why?'

'Because Mahesh believed in children.'

'Why?'

'What do you mean, why? You know surely that the Indian female is the personification of motherhood...at least in the eyes of the Indian male. He cannot imagine her wanting to be anything but a mother.'

'What did you want to be?'

'I don't know. I have such a lot of time...empty, vacuous. Sometimes I think I should become an actress... do my PhD...teach in a college...look after Mahesh's factory...stand for the Assembly...travel around the world...nurse the sick ...join a mission...write poems...'

'Show them to me.'

'What?'

'Your poems.'

'I don't write.'

'That's a lie.'

'I don't, honest...I just think about it.'

'Write.' He put a piece of paper before me.

'What?'

'Whatever comes to mind.'

I picked up the pen. It started to run on the paper. Sentences formed and were written...I kept laughing at myself throughout.

I live in moments
Spaced by desire
Wherein I am not
Sucked by melancholy deep in a hole
Imploding exploding
In a storm of hot dust
I ride the shoulder
Of my demented laughter
To leap out of the hole
With my last breath
And fall near you
I live again
The hole too I love
It is the only home I know
Deep deep in the hole
Down to the lowest depth
Where each moment implodes
Spewing lava and acrid smoke.

He read the lines, folded the paper and put it in his pocket.

'Send me whatever you write.'

'What if I don't write?'

'Impossible.'

'Don't curse me. I might end up writing a novel.'

'You will write, just as I will wander. If you were my wife, I might not have...'

'Why do you?'

'Everyone does.'

'No.'

'They do. Like the earth moving round the sun on an axis or without an axis. Imagine the condition of the earth if the sun were to disappear one day. It would wander here and there without direction like me, wouldn't it?'

'If there were no sun...'

'You understand why, if you were my wife, I would not have wandered all over the world.'

'Not ever?'

'Never, without you. First, we would have gone to Hong Kong...then Istanbul...Paris...Rome...'

'What about our half dozen kids?'

'Mahesh and Jenny could have brought them up.'

'Crazy.'

'It's perfectly sane. They were sure to have kids with or without us. Naturally, they and their respective spouses would have brought them up. From Rome we would have gone to China...then Japan...Australia... Jerusalem...'

'You mean you would have travelled all over the world and I would have moved round you like a satellite?'

'You could have stayed put like the sun in India and I would have moved round you every day like the earth.'

'Every day?'

'Every day. Every hour. Every second. The Earth is not allowed to stop.'

'Help! Day in and day out, you and only you! Morning and evening. Every morning. Every evening. At sunset and at sunrise. With the sun up at high noon... Mahesh would have passed by one day and I would have fallen in love with him.'

'I would have lost my sun and taken to tramping around the world. Its memory would have stayed with me, guiding me in my rambling. Now I wander because I yearn for something, propelled by passion. For what, I know not.'

'I might have made you more of a wanderer. You would have roamed the world trying to drown the pain of having chosen wrong.'

'No never.'

'Suppose it was so...'

'If you were my wife...come here...kiss me.'

'No.'

'Why not? I love you.'

'Don't. Let our love remain ephemeral.'

'If you were my wife...'

'No, Richard.'

'Kiss me once.'

'No.'

'I can kiss you.'

'No.'

'Why not?' he said but stayed where he was.

Time glided by...

'What happened?' I said.

'Only if you say, yes.'

'No, Richard.'

We stayed rooted where we were.

Time moved on...days and weeks passed...

We met at the club and parted...back where we started.

Time marched ahead...

If I were Richard's wife...if he were my husband...I would go to Japan with him, climb Mount Fujiyama... he would kiss me under the Eiffel Tower in Paris...if he went out of my life...if he left India never to return... if he returned but did not meet me...

Time moved on relentlessly. It did not stop for a second. Richard had come to India for eight months... he would go back after eight months...what if he never returned...or if he returned but I could not meet him?

A short rest on the deserted road stretching into

years…under the shade of a tall tree…a moment or two…for memory's sake…one kiss.

'Manu!' he said.

'What?'

'Nothing, just Manu.'

Time left us to ourselves.

'Manu!' he said.

'Yes.'

'Manu!'

'What?'

'Nothing, just Manu.'

Time stretched into a wilderness.

Parched months dragged by.

I took his face in my hands and kissed him.

'Manu!' he said.

'What?'

'Nothing, just Manu.'

We began to move with time. A tree began to flourish in the wasteland. Its lengthening shade took me in its embrace.

23

My first collection of poems arrived today.

I hold it in my hand. A black cover with splashes of red. Drops of blood spattered on the black sky of a dark monsoon night. Seeping blood shines even in the dark of the night.

What would be the colour of the sky stretching over Richard? Silver-grey, off-white, light blue, cobalt blue or dead black? Under how many skies oozing blood would I have to pass to reach him?

He had said send me whatever you write but... where?

My poems spanned ten years...No, Jenny tore those up...Richard was within my reach then! For years now, I have been collecting my poems in a coffin; five, six, perhaps seven...I used to count the days once, years pass now without count.

I stroke the cover of the book. Satin-smooth to the touch. Richard-Richard!

I had not lived through that moment of ecstasy for

ages. I closed my eyes, letting my hand glide over the smooth art paper...

Richard had a red mole in the middle of his back... wide and flat...easily held between two fingers...a patch of freckles on the right hip...the hand strayed there... back to the red mole...short steps braking on the slippery path...a depression in the curve of the shoulder.

'Made for your chin...' Richard had placed my chin there. My lips got lost in his thick hair; an earthy fragrance held me captive.

If I kept my eyes closed, I could still breathe it in.

'Sniffing the book?' Mahesh asked.

My eyes flew open.

'Fresh binding has a strange smell,' I said.

'Thrilling, is it?'

'Yes...no...?'

'To see your words in print?'

'Did you feel thrilled when you saw your factory?'

'Yes, I did.'

'Still do?'

'Not now.'

'Nor do I...now.' I laughed and gave the book to him.

He flipped it open.

To a gypsy, it said.

For Richard. Why not for Mahesh?

Why was it that only gypsies loved me...or was it me? Was it that I could only love a gypsy?

I am one of those people who live in moments. If I were to get love without a break, day after day, I was bound to feel bored. For someone like me, not getting was as important as getting; perhaps more.

I was one of those who had an infinite void within them, ready to absorb unhappiness. It was in our nature to invite gloom in, a symbol of our ego. When pain exceeds all bounds, we burst into laughter and leap out of the pit of melancholy. We live these moments of windfall freedom in ecstasy like the last moments of a prisoner condemned to death. Once the passion spends itself, we jump back in the pit.

Mahesh had turned over quite a few pages. He read in a low voice...

'Let us celebrate Independence Day
Hunger...unemployment...police atrocity
Newspaper rumours all
How can it happen,
When we are free...
He who belongs to no country
Sees slaves everywhere.'

'What can a lone man do?' Mahesh said.

He could do...a lot. A man who had no country of his own...he must be somewhere.

Richard, as long as you are, my not being does not hurt. If only you could see my book once.

I knew it would not reach him even if I sent it.

Jenny would never let him have it. For she would know: these are no poems, they are letters to him.

I have his permanent address in London. Actually, it is Jenny's address. Who knows where Richard would be at any time. How ludicrous to send my book to Richard at Jenny's address.

My laughing would not change anything...

My mind was busy churning out more letters. I would commit them to paper today, tomorrow or the day after. In a year, my second book will be ready. More poems bound in black...a coffin for my letters.

If only Richard could come for the celebration of the funeral...if only I knew where he was...if one more letter came from him...

Once...only once...

The publisher handed the book to me. There were others in the room. The book passed from one to the other.

'Good printing.'

'Artistic cover.'

'I don't care for art paper.'

'There is no option with black.'

'Only way to get gloss.'

'Red spattered on black...rather gaudy, don't you think?'

'Good for sales.'

'That's the main thing.'

'Colour cannot make poetry sell...red, yellow, whatever.'

'Who reads poems?'

'What if they were letters?'

'What do you mean?'

'Nothing.'

The publisher turned to me.

'Why poems? Why don't you write a novel? That's what sells.'

'One can read a novel while travelling.'

'Such a strain to read poems and so pointless.'

'What made you write poems?'

'They can be torn up more easily,' I said.

'What...?'

'Nothing.'

'What kind of a name is this?' a new entrant exclaims. 'Gypsy Passion? Too romantic.'

'Why do you people give such romantic names?'

'What's romantic, gypsy or passion?' I asked.

'Gypsy Passion...hmm...smacks of a western sensibility.'

'But the gypsies originated in India.'

'They were driven out ages ago. The West is their refuge now.'

'Suppose you said hippie instead of gypsy?'

'More contemporary.'

'No one talks of gypsies now.'

'What about passion?'

'What?'

'Nothing.'

Mahesh's friends had come for dinner.

Office talk was over. The political discussion didn't take off. Dinner was eaten. It was too early to break up. They needed something to talk about to break the monotony of half silences. 'Her book has come out.' Mahesh hit upon a topic. 'Whose? Mrs Goyal's? You mean you write?'

'...what do you write...poems...interesting hobby.'

'Well, you have the time to spare.'

'Two kids, Twelve and ten, quite grown-up.'

'So this is what you busy yourself with.'

'Not bad. Pass time and earn money from home. How much do you hope to get from this book?'

'A few kilos of white ants,' I said.

'What!'

'Nothing.'

A winter afternoon. Women from the neighbourhood gathered at my place.

'You never come out of your house. What do you do the whole day?'

'I'm having a sale of saris at Triveni. Please come.'

'Why don't you join our Ladies' Club?'

'We host coffee parties by turns. It is not all gossip, we learn things too. Why don't you...?'

'This book has your name on it!' One of them chances upon the book lying on the table. 'Have you written it?'

'Yes,' I had to admit.

'Let's see. So this is what you do.'

'Poems! Wow! We did not know you were a writer.'

'Hey listen! She writes.'

'If she is a writer she has to.'

'Come to our Ladies' Club one day. We should have a programme with her, no?'

'We can. She is from our colony.'

'Please come and read your poems one day. We believe in encouraging the arts.'

'But do keep refreshments, otherwise...'

'I'm sorry, I don't do readings,' I said.

'Why write then?'

'Because I can't roam around the world.'

'What do you mean?'

'Nothing.'

Richard, if only you could read my poems...once! After that, I would tear them up, one by one, page upon page. A thousand copies. Each with a hundred and forty pages. Not a bad way to spend time.

24

I have put time on a shelf against the wall. My fifth book arrived a few days ago. It joined the other four standing in attention in the glass-fronted bookcase. I never opened it. There was no need. A little dust managed to sneak in and settle on the books. I could peep through the glass and know five parts time was finished. My books were being published one after another. First poetry, then stories and finally novels.

'Don't curse me. I might end up writing a novel,' I had told Richard.

My publisher was right. Once my novel was published, my name became known to people.

'What does your name mean?' Richard had asked me once.

'It's a sound that comes from your lips and is sucked by my ears—that is meaning enough for me,' I had said.

My name on the book was a word, which would take forever to become a sound. Richard will not say it.

My hair was turning grey relentlessly. I did not have to search for the stray white any more.

The roots of the hair on both sides of the parting had gone completely white. Two serpentine footpaths.

'Let's look for footpaths,' Richard had said.

Footpaths were not parallel lines. They twisted and turned as they went on. Two persons travelling on separate paths could always hope to run into each other.

'...when...had thirty years passed?

Half of Richard's hair had gone grey but not fallen. It was as thick as ever. Copse of gold-grey strands. A silver thread gleamed in the eyebrows under the light.

Crow's feet planted by the side of the eyes.

Today I saw in the mirror, two more furrows had appeared on my face. From nose to lips. The cheeks sunk in their own pits on both sides. Lined trenches that meandered like white paths in his hair.

Richard was ageing, like me...he was growing old before his time...I was waiting.

There was a power cut since evening. I continued to sit before the mirror. I had turned the flame of a thick candle towards it. I did not feel like leaving the mirror. The room was in speckled darkness but for the mirror.

'Richard,' I said. 'My fifth book has come...do you want to see it?'

He smiled. The creases deepened.

'How many more will you write?'

'As long as you are...don't know how many.'

'Are you content?'

'No.'

'Happy?'

'No.'

'Proud?'

'No.'

'Tired?'

'Yes, tired enough to sleep.'

'What more do you want? Sleep at night and fatigue during the day?'

'Is that all there is to life?'

'Yes. Work during the day and rest at night.'

'But…writing books…is that work? What use are books?'

'Ask the readers.'

'You have not read them.'

'I know what is in them. Will you write more?'

'No…maybe…yes…'

What I am looking for is way down in the womb of the sand dunes.

Overhead, the sun spews fire…I gouge the desert sand with my nails…hot sand has scalded my fingers… ,my nails break with the digging…blood oozes out of the tips…what kind of a sun is this that never sets? What country is this that knows no night…no darkness … no sleep…for months? Perhaps I would get dizzy with exhaustion and leaving my search incomplete, I might fall asleep on the solitary sand dunes to sleep…and find another book on the shelf on waking up.

'I've just returned from the desert of Egypt,' I heard him say.

'Did you find anything?'

'Yes.'

'What?'

'Human beings.'

'They are everywhere.'

'Why are you searching then?'

'Richard!' I called out.

The mirror turned black. The barren desert got lost.

I am wandering in a dense forest…verdant, luxuriant, wild as far as the eye can see. Trees with lush creepers forming a fine mesh…bushes with thorns…merciless crowds…one got lost in a thick jungle as easily as in a barren desert…Is this crowd of…human beings or trees?

Hidebound trees, parasitical creepers climbing on others, bushes with thorns bared, grass that resists all trampling. When assailed, it bows its head, lies low, and survives.

Shall I too bow low, hug the grass, and lose myself in it? Will it rid me of my terrifying loneliness?

What kind of loneliness is this that clutches at me pulls me out of the crowd and never lets go?

I am looking for a way out. I flounder in the moss-encrusted grass and get sucked up to the knees. I reach out to cling to a branch but draw back wounded and bloodied with only a bunch of leaves in hand…thorns lurk under each leaf...my palms are pierced like a sieve...drops of blood ooze out slowly...sweat from every pore. Sullied and swooning, I would soon be nailed to a thorny bush and close my eyes.

I open them and find...one more book?

'I'm back from the jungle of Congo.'

'You penetrated it?'

'Yes.'

'What did you find?'

'More of the same...'

'Human beings?'

'Yes.'

'Richard, where will I find them in this crowd?'

Why doesn't he answer me? Why does the mirror turn black? Do I want an answer? Is blackness the only answer?

The mirror broke into pieces...

What an explosion! Soundless. No bang was heard. No flash was seen. No lava was thrown up. Only the mirror became full of splinters.

It did not fall to the ground. It broke into hundreds of pieces but remained stuck in the frame. Every piece in place. The cracked mirror projected a terrifying reflection of Richard. Not one with white hair on his head. All was gleaming golden. The face disintegrated, the wrinkles smoothened out.

I want him as he is today, white hair and wrinkles.

Whole. Not disintegrated like this. Richard-Richard! The candle flickered and went out. The room became pitch dark.

Richard, please. Say you are...somewhere... anywhere...in the deserts of Egypt...in the jungles of the Congo...on the glaciers of Iceland...you are... wherever you are...but you are...let me see you in my mirror once. Just once!

My eyes flew open in the silence of the night.

I felt someone enter the room. A cascade of light sprang out of the right corner. Even the shadow of some human forms beamed radiance.

This was such a form.

I could see it once I got used to the glow.

White cotton sari with plain border. Head covered with the sari end. Full-sleeved white blouse. Dress of a Bengali widow. Radiant beauty lighting up the wrinkled face.

I gazed at her steadily...the luminous shadow started moving back. I could not allow her to leave me like this. I must run and stop her.

'Mother Teresa! Mother Teresa!' I called with outstretched arms. The shadow merged in the wall. The singularly beautiful face gave an inviting smile. I put out my hand and tried to hold the edge of the white sari and...my eyes flew open.

There was no one in the room. I knew it was a

dream. I had it every night. I lived in a dream through the day and tried to find a way out of it at night. I know one should search for a place to reach, one should not simply choose a path suitable for wandering. Let me find the way, if not the destination. At least let me know which way to look and for what. I will search with the last breath of my life. I would breathe because I would have something to pursue.

Life without a quest has no meaning, Mother Teresa. Calcutta. Those destitute bastees where Richard had once worked.

We think of them after we have lost everything. We are small people. He who has everything, yet cares for them; he is the one to love?

Remember that astrologer, Richard, whom we met while wandering the streets of Delhi?

He had looked at my palm and said, 'You will either go mad or become a nun.'

You burst out laughing. 'Impossible. You will not go mad, nor will you become a nun.'

'Why not? What do you know about the future? For that matter, what do I know, and when we do not know, anything is possible.'

'Laugh once,' you had said.

'Why?' I had asked but laughed anyway.

'No, you will not go mad nor become a nun,' you had repeated.

'And you, I think, have already gone mad. Now you will tell me to cry and repeat, no, you will not go mad nor become a nun.'

'Cry,' you had promptly said.

I had really laughed then.

'Anyone who can laugh with such abandon cannot go mad or…'

'I heard. Stop chanting.'

Will you prove right? Will my laughter will save me? What would happen the day I know…you no longer are?

Is there no middle path, Richard?

If only I could go mad but not enough to be confined to a madhouse. Just demented enough to leave the house and take shelter in the sick bastees of Calcutta, to be a follower of Mother Teresa, without becoming a nun.

25

It was the month of August. It had been raining relentlessly for three days.

It was three in the afternoon. My room was dark like a cave. Darkness at noon is full of hazards. Darkness at night brings sleep; darkness in the day, dreams. All impediments seem to melt away.

The drops of rain were white like my hair. Behind them one saw the play of light and dark. Outside the rain was falling hard; dreams bloomed inside.

Suppose after all these years, Richard came today and stood at the threshold of my room…

The sky spewed ink…the rain silver…anything was possible.

It was a banyan tree—its canopy vast and spreading. We took shelter under it, not to escape the rain, but to rest a while, after getting drenched.

The sky was black as a cannon, the shade under the tree speckled.

The leaf canopy leaked. Drops of rain slithered like mercury from our faces to our bodies.

The rain was gaining in strength outside. We would get more soaked. I loved getting soaked by the rain.

'Have you ever bathed under the Niagara Falls?' he asked.

'Have you ever roasted corn on Mount Vesuvius?' I asked in return.

'When it rains in Cherrapunji, one feels one is under the Niagara Falls.'

'That way,' I laughed.

'Want to eat corn?'

'You have it?'

'No.'

'Then?'

'If we had corn, we could have roasted it on the fire...'

'If we had the fire.'

'If we had the corn...if you were not married, I would have married you...if I were not married.'

We laughed, drew closer. He kissed my wet face.

'Shall we light a fire?' he asked.

'In this rain?'

'Who needs a fire when it's sunny?'

'How would you light it?'

'Dig a pit. The earth would be dry underneath. Look amidst the roots of the banyan. You will find dry twigs. Pile them across one another. Rub two stones... but what would you eat?'

'You found nothing?'

'No. The game finds dark corners to hide in the twilight brought on by rain. Impossible to make a kill today.'

'Tomorrow?' I looked up.

'This is a banyan tree.'

'Why did we come here?'

'We are star-crossed lovers.'

'They will stone us to death.'

'If they catch us.'

'Don't light a fire.'

'Yes, fire has warmth but light too.'

'The light wipes out the shadows. We exist only as long as...'

The darkness grows in the room.

The rain patters drowsily outside.

Richard comes in stealthily.

'The sky is black like your hair,' he says.

I am astounded. In which era is he living...even today?

'Shall we light a fire?' he asks.

Yes, there is no need to be afraid. They have given up stoning lovers to death. Lovers have become civilised these days. They do not run away from society to take refuge in caves. Even when they transgress, they return to society's fold and surrender to a living death. As long as there was God, man sinned and put the responsibility of punishment on God. He managed to escape scot-free sometimes and sometimes got the indulgence to sin now but bear the punishment later, in another birth. The hidebound society was safe in its faith in God. When God died, man became responsible for everything. Society continued as it was because man civilised himself. Now when he rebels against society, he charges himself with the crime and pronounces sentence against himself. When we reach the zenith of civilisation, all our crimes will be committed in unison, with proper confabulation and mutual consent, to the sound of popular approbation. Was Germany not at the peak of its civilisation in 1939? As for England, it had become civilised centuries ago!

How then had Richard come back to me today?

'Shall we light a fire?' he asked again.

'If you are not afraid to.'

The fire blazed...or was it a flash of lighting...the rain shook itself awake.

'The rain falls in white streaks,' Richard said. 'Like your hair.'

The interval of time melted away...

Richard escaped from the prison of yesterday.

He folded me in a loose embrace in his limp arms and hid his wrinkled face in my lap. I began to stroke his silver hair.

I raised his face and filled the deep furrows on both sides of his nose with tips of my fingers.

He touched the fine net of wrinkles near my eyes and gathered the dapple grey shower of my hair in his hands.

Is that what lovers do when they meet after years? They read the footprints of time? Could dreams be that real?

Richard wet my lips with his tongue and asked, 'Have you ever bathed under the Niagara Falls?'

A banyan tree sprouted in the room, its canopy vast and spreading. The rain became a downpour. Lightning flashed repeatedly. Twilight shadows gathered under the banyan tree. The sky turned black like cannon; my hair dyed in its colour.

His lips moved. My body filled with warmth, lips scorched.

'Have you ever roasted corn on your lips?' he asked.

I crushed him in my arms. The wrinkles disappeared from his face. The grey abandoned the hair. The loose arms grew firm. They drew my feather-light body close...the lightning tactfully withdrew behind the clouds. The downpour drew a veil across us. Richard and I felt exonerated from all civilised crime and punishment.

'Sitting in the dark?' The light came on.

Mahesh loves the light. Light is his nature. He has not confronted darkness and even when he had to, he chose to look at the light.

'Why sit in the dark? You are not ill, I hope?' he said.

'It's noon.'

'But dark as night. What torrential rain. It was difficult to negotiate the roads. I had to take shelter under a tree.'

I closed my eyes. A banyan tree fanned out before me. Richard returned to my embrace. One could make the darkness one's own, however sharp the light outside.

'It's corn season,' I heard.

'Have you ever roasted corn on the Vesuvius?' I asked.

'What are you talking about?'

'Nothing.'

'Dreaming, were you?'

'Yes.'

'During the day?'

'The sun was tactful, it did not come out.'

'What was that?'

'Nothing.'

'Shall I make tea? You don't seem well.'

'I'm fine.'

'Were you asleep?'

'No, who can sleep in daylight?'

Even the darkness was not one's own; we had to share it.

'I'll get tea,' I said.

'I'd better change. My clothes are drenched,' Mahesh said.

'Yes, do. No need to light a fire.'

'What fire?'

'In the stove,' I said and burst out laughing.

Mahesh looked at me, surprised.

I switched my gaze to the electric light. I went to him, felt the wet sleeve of his shirt and said carefully, 'Go and change. I will go make tea. We have no coal, but we can roast the corn on the gas flame. I am sure the rain would soon stop. The sun would come out. The danger of darkness at noon will pass.'

I entered the kitchen. Lit the fire within the narrow, circumscribed limits of the gas stove. Put the pan of water on one flame and corncob on the other.

The rain still poured hard. The ink of the sky spilled into the kitchen. There was an iridescent dark around me. The only light came from the fire burning within the limits of the two circular flames.

The tea would brew, the corn get roasted...we would sit under the light to eat and drink together.

...I have little time...the darkness can be mine for a while longer.

I closed my eyes and reached the copious shade of the banyan tree...Richard was with me.

Share the light with others...the darkness may crack and splinter, but it would survive within you.

Epilogue

You who wanted to travel with me...

Look there in front of you. See the road turn the other way? Take that turn. Do not miss this opportunity. There is no exit after this. You would have to turn back. That would not feel nice, would it? No one wants to turn back in the midst of a journey.

See how curvaceous the turn is. It goes on to meet the Highway. Take it. Travel on the wide roads. May your journey be a joyous one!

You should leave now. To stay is to risk capture. Whoever lingers on this road ends up a vagabond, cursed to tramp forever. For this voyage has no end. You cannot see it right now but there is a solid wall blocking the way a little ahead. You have two options: bash your head on it or turn back.

Go forward and turn back...forward and back... aimless, unattached, in the unending wilderness of *shoonya*; walk and turn back...no prospect of rest...it is always high noon on this road.

A couple of trees that grew here have shrivelled. The glare of the sun is so intense it befuddles the vision. You can no longer see your whereabouts. One has to wander alone on this road...always.

Here...do what I tell you. Put your feet firmly on that turn of the road. If you continue with me, your persona will cease to exist. You are no longer visible to me. How can you be? I have no present, nor future. You did not exist in my past. I was alive only then, yesterday. I am not alive today but my yesterday is... he is not...but it is...

...what if I plant trees on this road... I might not have a future, which others do...

It is time for you to go. As for me, I have a job. I must plant trees along both sides of this desolate road, a tree for every moment shared, so that each moment will be enshrined in a tree. Come back after some years. This will be a road soft with the shade of trees.

You may sit in the shade of a tree if you wish and remember my story.

I have a request though. Please come only when this rambling journey of mine have come to an end...

ALSO IN SPEAKING TIGER

THE LAST EMAIL

A Novel

Mridula Garg

Almost forty years after the end of their passionate affair in New Delhi of the late 1970s, Kevin, a vicar devoted to the political struggle for Scottish independence, and Maya, a reputed author of Hindi literary works, re-establish contact—this time over email. As they slowly re-weave the delicate tapestry of their connection with each missive, they share the stories of their histories, interests, desires and despairs with each other. Ultimately, Kevin and Maya must realize, each on their own, whether the strength of their remembered passion can match the four decades of quotidian life they have both since accrued.

Written with grace and sensitivity, *The Last Email* is a moving account of two lives lived with passionate intensity, and steeped equally in love and in memory.